D1525127

HOMICIDE
AT
HIGH NOON

a Ghost Town mystery

Jamie L. Adams

On the advisement of my twins, I'd like to dedicate this book to a cat named Bug (short for Lovebug) and the wonderful people who love her. Abandoned, Bug came to live with us when she was just ten days old. My daughter, Amber, cared for her and taught the kitten everything a mother cat would, just not always in the same fashion. My daughter, Crystal, spoils Bug like only an aunt can and, of course, there's Grandpa Rick, who Bug adores. Thanks, Bug, for converting me from a non-pet person to a cat lover.

I'd also like to thank the wonderful people who helped me get Ghost Town Mysteries from an idea to a series. My agent, Dawn, without whom none of this would have been possible, Gemma, the amazing wind beneath my wings, and the talented editors whose skills make it all read so much better.

CHAPTER ONE

"Go down in flames."

———

"Stay still!"

Startled by the rapid-fire command directed at me, I stopped swinging my legs and looked up. The jagged scar on the left cheek of the tall, dark haired man's face creased with excitement. A devious grin flashed across his rugged features, and for a split second, my brain contemplated going into a fight or flight response.

From where I sat, flight was not possible, so I raised my hand to shade the bright, November sun from my eyes and hesitantly asked, "What?"

The smile on his face spread into a wide grin, sending an icy cold shiver down my spine when I realized what he intended to do. Me and my bright ideas. How had I ever let myself get into this situation?

"We're going for a ride," his deep voice boomed in the crisp autumn air. The message his words conveyed sent my heart into a panic.

"Wait." I struggled to recall his name, although earlier I'd thought how ironic it was that his spiked hair and the gap between his front teeth resembled a character with the same nickname from a cartoon I'd watched recently with my niece and nephew.

Another man, operating the hinged safety gates on the raised platform, pressed a button, and the metal partition beneath us dropped. My stomach *whooshed* as I felt myself falling from the one-hundred-and-fifty-foot-high platform. A scream stuck in my throat, and my arms tensed as I held on to the overhead handlebars with an ironclad tight grip.

"Relax," he shouted from somewhere beside me, on the other set of the parallel cables holding us in the air.

A gust of wind whipped a section of dark brown hair across my brow, and it took me a moment to realize I had my eyes closed. I let go with one hand long enough to brush the wayward curls from my vision and then looked over to my right. Buckled into a seat beside me, the instructor waved. He wore a proud grin, and the look of joy in his eyes helped settle my nerves while he motioned for me to look down.

Under our feet, a canopy of treetops filled my vision as we soared above the wilderness expanse. The view was a breath-taking sight! From here in the sky, you could see everything. Roads, rivers, wildlife, people, even the birds had nowhere to hide from our spectacular vantage point.

The Ward County National Park's zip line ride had been the first on my list of nearby attractions to visit, and from the start, I had been sold. Well, after the initial shock of stepping out into space strapped to a rope. The certified instructor, Doug, that was his name, should have been a sales agent. Since the Calico Rock Mine and Ghost Town's planning committee liked the idea of adding a zip line to The Park's activities, they needed information on price, upkeep, and safety issues. As The Park's manager, I was on a field trip gathering information.

Too soon, we reached the bottom of the ride. My cheeks felt cold from the autumn air and flushed with the adrenaline racing through my body. "My sisters are going to be so jealous." I said the first thing that came to mind as Doug showed me how to unbuckle from the contraption.

"We're open six days a week." He pulled a business card from his shirt pocket and handed it to me. "Tell them to come on down—or up, that is."

I chuckled at his humor and promised to pass the word to my family before heading toward the parking lot where I'd left my Jeep Wrangler. My steps were wobbly at first, but after a few strides, I had my land legs back.

Adding a zip line to The Calico Rock Mine and Ghost Town would allow our guests to enjoy the Old West from a whole new perspective. The rustic buildings, dusty roads, and boardwalks would resemble an old western movie set when viewed from above. Starting from the top of the cliff above the gold mine to the east and ending on the grassy plateau beside the river west of the entrance would provide a spectacular view of our Wild West themed attraction park.

Tempted to pinch myself, I hummed as I climbed into the Jeep and started the engine. Seven months ago, I'd been managing a large campground in the Ozarks. After five years of living with chiggers, ticks, and high humidity, I'd been eager to return home to California. When Steve, The Park's chairman of the board, called to offer me a job, I had jumped at the chance. Managing the ghost town associated with my hometown of Grady had been my dream from the start of my career. Living at home again with my sisters, family and friends nearby was almost too good to be true.

The thirty-minute drive back to work took me through Placerville, the only other town within a fifty-mile radius, which had my favorite fast-food restaurant. Feeling hungry, I pulled into the drive-thru to order a chicken sandwich and an iced tea for lunch. Thankfully, I was able to find a nice shade tree to park under while I enjoyed my meal. My phone buzzed as I unwrapped the food, and I glanced at the caller ID. Pat, my older sister, was calling, so I swiped the screen and put the volume on speaker before setting it beside me on the console.

"Hello, Pat," I said and then dipped a curly fry into the ketchup container I'd requested along with my meal.

"Lily, are you at work?" She sounded short of breath, which was out of the ordinary for my calm and collected sibling. My younger sister, Ava, was the emotional one who grew excited over the simplest things, such as a redbird landing on a tree branch or being able to make out a face in the clouds, but Pat, not so much.

I took a sip from my drink and washed down a mouthful of fries. "No, why?"

"It's nothing, really." A sigh of relief resonated in her voice. "I just had a funny feeling and thought of you."

I set aside my tea and picked up the phone. "Are you all right?"

"Of course, I'm fine." She let out a short laugh as if my question were silly and then cleared her throat. "Where are you?"

"On my way back from Ward County," I said. She knew about my touring different zip lines in the area to get a feel for which type would best suit The Park. Who knew there was more than one to choose from? "Remember, I was going zip-lining."

"That's right." Pat paused, and I wondered if she really had forgotten. It wasn't like my sister to forget anything. The self-imposed matriarch of our family now, she ran a tight ship when it came to schedules. "How did you like it?"

"The ride was fabulous!" I snuck another bite of my sandwich before the chicken got cold. "You and Jack should take the kids one day. They'll love it."

The twins were eleven and a half and always up for adventure. Jack Owens, my sister's husband, could use a break from his job at the sheriff's department. Serving as the sheriff of Ward County, he rarely got time off, although the idea of his over six-foot frame soaring down the line made me want to giggle. I wasn't so sure he'd enjoy the adventure as much as the kids.

"Well, let me talk it over with Jack first," she said with a large dose of caution. "Before we say anything about taking a zip line ride to the twins."

After we hung up, I finished eating my meal and then checked the time. I needed to head back to The Park. Gretchen Thompson, our office manager, could hold down the fort while I was gone, but I still liked to be available in case something needing my attention came up. When I pulled onto the property, the day's activities were in full swing. SUVs and recreational vehicles packed the parking lot. The Calico Rock Mine and Ghost Town had been having exceptional crowds ever since last summer when we discovered a new vein of gold in the old, abandoned mine. Tourists meandered down Main Street, taking in the original false front buildings built over one hundred years ago. We had upgraded the structures to meet safety standards while keeping the authentic appearance, and we only used material available from the days of the town's creation.

Character actors, dressed in costumes, interacted with the crowd while playing the part of someone from the gold rush era. Sheriff Tom tipped the edge of his Stetson as he passed me on the boardwalk. The spurs on his leather boots tapped out a rhythm with each step he took. Last September, we'd added a genuine refurbished stagecoach to circle through the town every hour on the hour. Pulled by two black Morgan horses, Duke, and Dolly, who when not working were kept corralled next to the blacksmith's barn, the new ride was a great addition. I'd ridden in the coach once. The interior was too dark for my liking, and the closed confines made me feel claustrophobic, but the kids loved it.

When I entered the office, Gretchen greeted me with a tight smile, and my steps slowed. The tall, thin, bleached blonde always wore a bright, cheerful expression on her face, but this one looked strained and forced. Beside the receptionist's desk stood Steve, the bank president and chairperson of The Park's planning committee. Next to him, a tall, thin man I'd never seen before sneered in my direction. His thick dark hair and bushy eyebrows paled when compared to his Fu Manchu style mustache. His dark hair wove around the corners of his mouth until it reached the end of his chin. Short and stout, Steve's clean-shaven face looked naked next to the stranger. Neither of them appeared pleased to see me.

"Good afternoon." The hardened look in Steve's eyes did not bode well. "Lily, this is Melvin Rinehart, from the Rinehart Accounting Firm. He also serves as the bank's auditor."

"Hello." I reached out to shake his hand, but instead of taking mine, he handed me a business card with the name Melvin J. Rinehart printed in gold lettering over a glossy maroon background. Concerned they'd think I'd been playing hooky from work, I said the first thing that came to my mind. "I've just returned from trying out one of the nearby zip lines."

My words didn't sound as reasonable an explanation as I had hoped, so I dug the hole deeper by babbling. "I never knew how great a place Ward County's National Park is to visit."

"Let's go into your office." Steve tilted his head toward the hallway leading to the back of the building.

"Sure. Follow me," I said and then led the way to the room not much larger than a walk-in closet, set aside to serve as the park manager's private office. Thanks to the help of my sisters, we'd made the tiny quarters as cozy as possible. I sat down in the upholstered black captain's chair behind my desk, and the two men took a seat on the chairs across the room from me.

After they were settled, Steve got right to the point of this unplanned meeting. "Melvin is the bank auditor, and we've asked him to look into The Park's banking accounts."

"Oh, I see," I said, although I really didn't. Still, I believed it was good practice to keep company funds in check.

"There seems to be a discrepancy in spending," he continued, and my heart sank. Not too long ago, The Park had been struggling to stay open. We'd worked so hard to cut back on spending and keep the numbers out of the red. I'd believed the recent discovery of gold on the property had put all our money troubles behind us.

"What do you mean?" I asked sharply. The fact they'd called in an auditor seemed to imply something more serious than a simple mathematical error in bookkeeping.

"Someone has withdrawn a large amount of money from the account," Mr. Rinehart explained with more than a hint of accusation in his tone. "And there's no receipt to show what they used the funds for."

"When we looked deeper, we noticed strange activity on more than one occasion," Steve added in a stern yet less threatening tone. "And there will need to be an investigation."

My stomach stiffened like a ball of tightly wound rubber bands. What were they suggesting? From the sound of it, they suspected me of taking the missing money, but Steve knew me better than that. We'd grown up in the same small town. My father and his dad had been fishing buddies. Our mothers had helped organize bingo games at the civic center on Wednesday nights. I wasn't some stranger off the street.

Calm down, Lily. My mother's gentle voice whispered in my ear, as if she'd risen from her final resting place to comfort her high-strung daughter. *It's the curse of being the middle child*, she'd often told me when I had fretted over a seemingly big ordeal as a teenager, but long since forgotten now.

"I can assure you I have not been taking money from the account for myself." I swung around to face my computer and, like a woodpecker on steroids, tapped the keys to log into The Park's banking information. "Can you give me the amount and date?"

Steve pulled out his phone and used his index finger to scroll as he looked for the information. "On September 7th, someone withdrew $1000 from The Park's account, but there is no record of what we used the money for. Does the amount sound familiar to you?"

"No," I said and stopped typing. There was no need to look any further. Although necessity had forced us as a company to dip into the reserves last summer to pay bills, we never touched the special account now since the mine was back in full operation. Such a large amount taken without a receipt looked highly suspicious and required the attention of an accountant from the outside. Hence, Mr. Melvin J. Rinehart.

My brain was still whirling in overdrive on the way home after work. Why was it when everything was going better than I had ever dreamed, the bottom threatened to fall out? I kept my attention on the road while blinking moisture from my eyes.

"I can't believe they suspect you of doing such a thing." My sister, Ava, sat in the passenger seat with her arms crossed at her waist. Her hazel eyes narrowed and a short huff slipped through her tight lips. I'd told her what had taken place that morning, and she was still grumbling by the time we got home. "You saved the mine, and this is how they repay you?"

I hadn't saved the mine, but we had discovered there was more gold waiting to be dug out under my watch, so to speak. Pat, Jack, and the twins were at the farm when we pulled into the driveway. A family dinner night on the worst day of my life was not something I needed. To say I was a hot mess was putting it mildly. Angry, confused, and terrified all mixed in one, I wasn't up to being a fun aunt or even behaving socially acceptably.

Pat and her crew showed up once or twice a week to make dinner for everyone. She was big on planning ahead, but from time to time would surprise us. Although Ava and I were the only ones living in the large two-story house, Cranston Acres was as much Pat's as ours. Once a dairy farm, the twenty acres of land were now rented out to a rancher, but the homestead itself served as the center of our family activities. All three of us girls had grown up helping Dad milk the cows and Mom bake bread. The family homestead was a few miles outside the Grady city limits, and we'd lived a charmed life.

Two years older than me, Pat had married the local high school football star turned sheriff, and they had eleven-year-old twins, Jack Jr., and Jill, who'd been named after our mother and not a children's nursery rhyme. Widowed after less than two years of marriage to her high school sweetheart, Ava Ashton nee Cranston was the baby of our family. I, on the other hand, had chosen a different path by going to college and moving out of state, but recently, I'd returned home to become the manager of the Calico Rock Mine and Ghost Town, better known by the locals as The Park.

When Ava and I stepped into the living room, a whiff of roast beef and cooked vegetables wafted in from the kitchen. Mom's favorite meal. If only she were still alive. One of her hugs would have done the trick right about now. She'd always had a way of making things feel less scary.

Both redheaded and freckled-faced, the twins looked up from the L-shaped black leather sectional couch, where they sat playing on their electronic devices. The furniture in the house was outdated, but thirteen years after the death of our parents, none of us had the heart to toss out what held so many dear memories.

Jack Jr. cupped his hands around his mouth and looked toward the kitchen. "The aunts are here," he yelled as if calling out a warning.

"Quick, someone get the bug spray," Ava teased, and we all smiled. Some jokes never grew old.

"Dinner will be ready soon," Pat called out from the other room. "But you still have enough time to change."

Working at The Park required us to wear a western period costume. Donned in our long dresses with matching bonnets, Ava and I both looked fresh off the wagon trail. By Pat suggesting we change our clothes before we eat, she meant she'd invited Cody West to dinner. The local crime scene investigator was a close friend of the family, and both my sisters fixated on pairing the two of us as a couple. To be honest, I'd grown fond of the idea even though, now widowed for over a decade, Cody had been married to one of my best friends from high school. Although I was pretty sure Cody felt the same way about me, when he found out I was the prime suspect in an embezzlement investigation, he'd have every right to change his mind.

By the time I'd put on a pair of jeans, my favorite blue V-neck blouse, and returned to the living room, Cody sat on the couch looking at a video Jill had on her phone. If I knew my niece well, the pictures had something to do with cats. She wanted a kitten of her own more than anything. A new pet topped her Christmas wish list. Our cat, Cocoa, sat in between the two of them curled in a ball. Cody slowly stroked the sleeping feline's back. The man's natural good looks and pensive dark brown eyes had caught my attention way back when we were kids in school together.

"Good evening," I said when I entered the room. Cody raised his focus from the video, returned my greeting with a warm smile, and then stood. Tall with dark brown hair that matched his eyes, the man's toned body and chiseled good looks would fit right in on the cover of a magazine.

"Hello," he said, and even though we'd known each other for years, that deep voice of his still did things to my insides.

"Dinner's ready." Pat called from the dining room, where she had the food on the table.

With one side of his mouth raised in a playful grin, Cody placed a hand on his waist, dipped his chin, and made a sweeping gesture with his free arm toward the dining room before giving me a long, slow wink. "After you."

Thank goodness the kids were behind him. By all indications, the two of them were in on their mother's matchmaking scheme. They would have hooped and hollered like a pair of outlaws who'd gotten away with robbing the Lone Star Saloon on a Saturday night if they'd glimpsed anything suggesting a romantic relationship between the two of us. For a split second, all thoughts of my horrible day slipped away.

I'd waited until we'd finished eating to share my bad news. It was something we'd learned from our dad. There was no sense in getting the family upset before a meal over something that could wait for a better time. The kids had gone down to the basement with Ava to check out a new game on her laptop while I joined Pat, Jack, and Cody in the living room.

"All right." Pat waited until I'd taken a seat beside Cody on the sofa. His woodsy cologne and the smell of peppermint were uniquely him. He had a fondness for hard candy and wore Old Spice. I found the combination and his presence reassuring. Sitting across from us, Pat leaned forward and pinned me to the wall with one of her piercing looks. "Tell us what's wrong."

Hiding my emotions was something I'd never done well, so I got right to the point. "Steve thinks someone has been taking money from The Park's account and has called for an audit."

Of course, my statement got Jack's full attention. Embezzlement was the sort of thing that would be of interest to the county sheriff. He set down his drink and glanced at Cody for a moment before giving me his sternest raised brow look. "Does he have any idea who?"

"No," I said hesitantly because, although they didn't know who took the money, the owners of the company had their eyes on one person—me. "There are only a handful of people who have access to The Park's primary account, but even then, the funds are only disbursed after approval by the planning committee."

"So, the missing money came from The Park's primary account?" Cody placed his left hand on the narrow empty space on the couch between us and lightly tapped his fingers against the cushion. Tempted, I refrained from slipping my hand in his for moral support. Not because I'd done anything wrong, but because no one enjoyed being falsely accused of a crime.

"Yes," I said. My voice squeaked, so I took a sip from my tea glass and then licked my dry lips.

"That was a pretty bold and a stupid move for a thief or an embezzler to make." Jack shook his head in disbelief.

"It's like they didn't care if they got caught," I agreed. "Or they were pretty sure they wouldn't be discovered."

"Or didn't realize how easy it would be to trace the transaction," Cody added.

"I'm confused," Pat said, which must have been hard for her to admit.

"The Park's money goes into a primary account," I explained. "And then gets disbursed into smaller accounts meant to cover different areas of operation like maintenance, wages, and insurance, just to name a few."

She still looked confused, so I tried to explain in more detail. "I keep track of expenses and let the committee know where the money is needed most and then the funds are moved to cover expenditures."

"Ah." She nodded while a look of understanding spread across her face. "If money is taken out before being moved to another account, it's a big red flag."

"Yes," I said, impressed with how easily she'd summarized the situation.

"So, why don't they just go to the person who has access to the primary account and ask them what they did with the money?" Before she'd finished the question, her face paled, and she pressed the tips of her fingers against the space above her top lip. "They think you did it."

"In theory, I'm the only one who would have any business being in that account." My voice shook, and I felt my chin tremble. Cody's firm, warm hand clasped mine and squeezed gently.

CHAPTER TWO
"Someone woke up on the wrong side of the bed."

––––––––––

The next morning, I got out of bed earlier than usual because I hadn't slept well from all the tossing and turning as I contemplated serving time in prison for a crime I hadn't committed. My family and Cody had assured me everything would work out in the end, but I wasn't so sure. Something about the eager expression on the bank auditor's face had set me on edge. Beady eyed, he'd looked like a shark about to pounce on its next meal.

While getting ready for work, I'd just finished lacing up my tall leather boots when the phone rang. A number I didn't recognize appeared on the screen, and I considered not answering, even though it was kind of early in the day for a telemarketer to be calling. By the third ring, I gave in to my insatiable curiosity and answered, "Hello?"

"Miss Cranston," a nasally male voice droned in my ear. "This is Melvin Rinehart."

"Good morning." I kept my voice as cheerful as possible, which wasn't easy considering the circumstances. "How are you, Mr. Rinehart?"

"I need to see you in my office today," he demanded without any sort of greeting or bothering to answer my question.

"All right," I said with confidence, as I had nothing to hide and wanted to get this over with. "How about I stop by on my way to The Park this morning?"

"No," his voice rose with indignation, as if I'd suggested an outlandish time to meet. "This morning isn't convenient for me."

If that were the case, he could have waited and called me at the office. I wasn't sure if he was playing head games or on some sort of power trip. Maybe both.

"Okay," I said with composed restraint. "What time would be good for you?"

After a brief pause, I heard him clear his throat and then of all things he said, "I'll call you later this morning at the office and let you know."

Talk about feeling dumbfounded. This man was turning a terrible mistake into a nightmare. Whatever happened to innocent until proven guilty?

"What is this all about?" I didn't mean to sound so challenging, but the bank's accountant was getting on my nerves. Considering our positions, I dialed my attitude back a few notches by adding, "I mean, I know what it's about, but why the sudden urgency?"

"We'll talk later," was all he said before he hung up.

Mr. Melvin Rinehart was a strange man. His name was familiar to me as one of Grady's well-established accountants, but other than that, I knew nothing about him. I guess I needed to conduct a little investigation of my own.

"Lily?" Ava called from downstairs.

I glanced at the radio clock on the nightstand beside my bed. If I didn't hurry, we'd be late for work. Fridays were her favorite day playing the part of the Calico Rock School teacher, and she liked to take treats to work with her to celebrate the end of another week. Last night, she'd baked a pan of frosted fudge brownies to hand out to the children visiting her station at the one-room schoolhouse.

I hustled down the stairs and went straight to the kitchen. "We better hurry or we'll be late," I said as I grabbed an apple and rushed for the door.

Ava sounded like she was out of breath by the time she climbed into the passenger seat of my Jeep. She set the brownies on the dashboard while taking a moment to buckle her seat belt. I turned on the engine and put my foot on the brake. "Ready?"

"Yes," she said and grabbed the food before it ended up on the floor. "You seem upset. Is something wrong?"

"Mr. Rinehart called while I was getting dressed." I shifted into reverse with more force than required and then twisted my torso to look over my shoulder as I backed out of the driveway. "He wants to see me this afternoon."

"Well," she said in a soft voice, no doubt trying to get me to take it easy. "You had to know it was going to happen, eventually."

"Yes," I agreed and took a deep breath to calm my nerves. "But he didn't have to be so rude about it."

"I've never met him." Ava stared out the passenger window as we drove past the high school. An online tutor when not working at The Park, I wondered if she'd prefer teaching in a classroom. She let out a sigh and turned her attention toward me. "But he has a reputation for being hard-nosed."

"Now I know why." I slowed down to cross the railroad tracks and then turned left onto First Street. The Park was a few miles outside of town. Both of us lost in our own thoughts, we remained quiet for the rest of the drive.

"Are you going to be all right?" Ava asked when we pulled into the employee parking lot.

"Don't worry about me," I assured her with a cynical smile while quoting one of our mother's favorite sayings and the theme from my relatives last night, "Everything will work out."

The words came out sounding as sarcastic as I meant for them to. Ava patted my shoulder and then stepped out of the vehicle. We hiked up to the entrance without speaking until we'd reached the hand painted welcome sign on the other side of the footbridge.

"You know where to find me if you need to talk," Ava said with a gentle smile. My sweet younger sister, she took after Mom more than any of us.

"Thanks." Cringing at the sound of my voice cracking, I ducked my head and headed for the office. I had promised myself I would not cry today.

Gretchen was sitting at her desk when I entered the lobby. One of the few employees whose job allowed them to come to work in normal clothing, she had on a turquoise blouse and matching miniskirt, with a long silver necklace and silver belt. A frown marred her usually bright smile.

"Good morning." I greeted her with a friendly grin since I refused to let this dark cloud hanging over us ruin my day.

"Melvin Rinehart wants to speak with you." She pointed toward the phone. "He's been on hold for a while."

"I'll take it in my office," I said after checking the clock. I wasn't late. He was being obnoxious. I'd known this man for less than twenty-four hours, and already he was one of my least liked individuals. I took my time getting settled into the chair behind my desk.

"Ms. Cranston," His voice rang with disapproval once I connected the call. "I'll expect to see you in my office at twelve."

"Sure," I said. "I'll plan on being there during my lunch break."

"Don't be late," he snapped and then hung up.

For the next three and a half hours, I stayed holed up in my office doing paperwork. Thankfully, there weren't any calls requesting a tour. I would have asked one of the backup guides to take my place if anyone had wanted to be shown around The Park.

Determined to be at the accountant's office door right at twelve on the dot, I left before Gretchen returned from her lunch break. After I put the *Out to Lunch* sign on the door, I locked up and jogged to the employee parking lot. Ten minutes before the appointed time, I pulled the Jeep Wrangler into a space in front of the tall two-story brick business complex. According to the sign in front of the building, there was a barber shop and a hair salon besides Mr. Rinehart's accounting office. A white slide-out panel had the words *Remodeled Rental Space Available Soon* in bold black letters.

There was a long walkway that divided the well-maintained lawn, with low-lying shrubs on either side of the narrow cobblestone path. A coin on the ground glinted in the sunlight, so I stooped to pick it up. It looked like a buckwheat penny. Focused on the upcoming meeting, I scarcely glanced at the coin before I dropped it into my purse. Ava got a kick out of adding them to the collection our father had started years ago. I reached the double glass doors at the same moment Sam Smith stepped outside. A smile spread across the barber's face as he held the door for me. "Good afternoon, Miss Lily."

I'd known Sam since I was a little girl. My sisters and I used to tease our dad about his bald barber. When I was a kid, sometimes Dad would take me to town when he was having his hair cut. I remembered looking forward to the suckers Sam kept in a tall glass jar for my sisters and me. He'd claimed they were only for us, but I suspected he handed them out to other children as well. When the time came for Dad to get his hair cut, he and Sam had talked like they were the best of friends and had known each other for years. The barber shop had always been a comfortable place for me to visit and brought back wonderful memories.

"Hello, Sam," I said with heartfelt warmth as I passed over the threshold and entered the building. "How are you doing?"

"I'm doing simply fine. Thank you," he said, still wearing his barber's apron. Sam seemed to be in a hurry, and he sounded a bit out of breath but paused long enough to add, "It's nice to see you again, Lily."

By the time the door shut behind me, Sam had reached the sidewalk, headed for an old rusted out red truck. The building's lobby sign showed the accountant's office was on the second floor. Giving myself a mental pep talk, I made my way up the stairs to Mr. Rinehart's office.

At the top of the landing, I paused long enough to take a deep breath to build up my courage to see the man who seemed to thrive on intimidating people. The office space on the opposite side of the building was empty inside except for a ladder and long strips of clear plastic hanging from the ceiling. The remodeling work had a way to go before they'd be ready to put it up for rent. Plaster and dust covered the carpet. It surprised me that Mr. Rinehart allowed the carpenters to leave such a mess.

While frowning at the condition of the walkway, I took another deep breath and knocked on the outer door to Mr. Rinehart's office. No one answered, so I stepped inside to find a small waiting room with plastic green ferns, three tan straight-back chairs, and a glass top coffee table with old magazines. On the other side of the room, there was an empty receptionist's table and chair. The absence of any sign of paperwork or a computer led me to believe the accountant did not have a receptionist. A large oak door with a brass plate identified Melvin T. Rinehart's private office.

"Mr. Rinehart?" No one answered my call, so I crossed the room and tapped lightly. Someone had left the door open a fraction.

"Hello?" I called out and knocked a little louder. He didn't answer. *What kind of game was this man playing?*

Irritated by the accountant's hurry up and wait tactics, I pushed the door open wide enough to enter and stepped into the room. Mr. Rinehart wasn't sitting at the desk, and his tall leatherback chair leaned at an odd angle. I moved across the room until I reached the large oak tabletop covered with files and a computer. On the other side of the desk was the accountant, face down on the ground with a large green marble paper weight on the floor beside him.

Oh, no. Not again.

My mind raced back to last summer, and my stomach churned. I knelt beside him and felt for a pulse. Nothing. Had he had a heart attack and fallen? The heavy weight beside him looked suspicious. Red streaks on the base of the oversized chess piece looked a lot like blood. While still kneeling, I glanced around the room. Tall bookshelves filled too tight to hold another book, the large oak desk loaded with files, and a nice swivel office chair. Across the room stood a large file cabinet next to an open door, revealing a private bathroom.

My blood ran cold. What if I wasn't alone? The person who had done this to Mr. Rinehart could easily be hiding. After taking a moment to consider my options, I rose and tiptoed toward the darkened room. With a shaky hand, I flipped on the light and looked inside. The small room was empty other than a few personal items on the counter next to the sink, like an expensive beard and mustache grooming kit and a comb.

Relieved to know whoever might have killed the accountant had apparently left the building, I went back to the waiting room and pulled out my phone to call my brother-in-law, Jack. Most people would have dialed 9-1-1 in this type of emergency, but there was no helping Mr. Rinehart now, and I had the head of the sheriff department's private number.

"Hello," Jack answered on the second ring. He sounded preoccupied but not bothered by my calling him in the middle of the workday.

"Jack," my voice shook, and it took me a second to continue. I'd been fine until the moment it came time to say the words aloud. "The accountant is dead."

There was a brief silence and then came his confused reply, "Lily?"

Of course, Jack didn't know what I was talking about. As far as he knew, I was at The Park, playing a character from the Old West. I took a deep breath to calm my nerves and explained, "I had an appointment to meet with Mr. Rinehart, but when I got here, he was on the ground, not breathing."

"Did you call an ambulance?" Jack asked. I heard what sounded like a drawer shutting and a chair pushed across hardwood flooring.

"No, it's too late for that." I wasn't a trained medical professional, but I'd seen enough dead bodies to know one when I came across one. This wasn't the first time I'd seen a lifeless body outside of a funeral parlor. "He's dead."

"I'll be right there," Jack said and then, after a brief pause, asked, "Are you at his office now?"

"Yes," I said. As much as I wanted to go, I knew better than to leave the scene before the authorities arrived. "I'm in the waiting room."

"Is anyone else there?" Jack's breathing sounded labored, as if he were walking fast.

"No, I'm alone," I said, glancing around the room. I heard what sounded like Jack shutting a car door and then the muffled roar of an engine revving up.

"Stay in the waiting room," Jack ordered before adding, "and Lily, make sure you don't touch anything."

After we hung up, I made myself as comfortable as one could make themselves on one of the straight-back chairs, knowing there was a dead body in the next room. Not sure what to do while I waited, I looked around the room. Someone had left a wrinkled gum wrapper in the fake soil of the green plastic planter next to me. The phony fern stood tall and remarkably clean of dust. Mr. Rinehart had kept a clean yet bleak office.

My attention wandered to the door of his private quarters. A man in his position struck fear in his subordinates, and he couldn't have had too many friends, not with that superiority complex of his. I didn't want to jump to conclusions, but the likelihood of that paperweight somehow falling from a shelf and striking him on the head seemed a bit far-fetched. Had he been alone when he'd called me a few hours ago? I raked my memory but could not recall having heard any background noise when we spoke on the phone. He hadn't sounded upset or nervous either. Far from it, he'd given me the impression he was ready to make a killing himself.

I didn't have to wait long for Jack to arrive, considering the sheriff's station was less than five miles away. He arrived in under ten minutes. What I hadn't expected was to see Cody following Jack into the accountant's office. I shouldn't have been surprised since he was the crime scene investigator for our county. If the situation weren't so serious, I would have found their matching expressions comical. They both had surprised deer in the headlights looks on their faces.

"Is he in there?" Jack asked as he strolled across the room and marched into Melvin Rinehart's inner office like he owned the place.

I stood and started to follow him, but Cody placed his hand on my arm. The warmth in his dark brown eyes gleamed with genuine concern. "Are you okay?"

"Yes, I think so," I said and let him lead the way to the doorway, where I watched the two men examine the crime scene.

Speaking in low voices, they crouched beside the body on the other side of the room. Their muttering made it impossible to decipher the gist of their conversation. Cody rose, pulled out his cell, and started making calls. Jack came to stand beside me. "Did you touch anything?"

It took me a moment to recall if I had or not. "No, I didn't. Do you think he was murdered?"

"There's a gash on the back of his head," he said with a nod.

I shuddered at the thought of someone hitting the accountant over the head, hard enough to kill him. "I spoke with him on the phone not long before I arrived."

"What about?" Jack pulled out his notepad and pen.

"He called to tell me what time I should come by to see him." It wasn't necessary for me to explain why the accountant wanted to see me. Jack knew.

"Did he say anything that might have indicated he was in distress at the time you spoke on the phone?" Jack asked.

"No," I said, thinking back to our conversation. "He sounded fine."

Jack's gaze roamed the waiting room. "Was there anyone else in the office when you entered?"

"No, I let myself in when no one answered my knock on the door," I explained. "The inner office door was open slightly."

Jack gave the aforementioned door a curious look when a team of investigators entered the main office and continued toward the crime scene. We had to step aside to let them pass.

"Did you notice anyone suspicious hanging around the building?" he asked while writing something on his notepad.

"No," I said, wishing I could be more helpful. "The only other person I saw in the building was Sam."

"Sam?" Jack looked up from his note taking.

"You know." I wrinkled my nose in surprise because everyone in town knew Sam Smith. "The barber."

Jack nodded and jotted something down. "What was he doing?"

"He held the door for me when I entered the lobby." I explained. "He was on his way out, and I didn't see anyone else in the building."

The complex had two businesses on the first floor. There was The Clip and Dye, a hair salon owned by Ava's friend Chloe Brown and then Sam's Barbershop. They were on the same side of the lobby next to each other. On the second floor there were two larger offices, Mr. Rinehart's and an empty one across the hall. While the accountant's office was behind enclosed walls, they had left the other office exposed due to remodeling.

After I'd told Jack everything I knew, he let me go. I stepped out of the accountant's office and let out a weary sigh. On my way down the stairs, I spotted Sam Smith slip into the barbershop. Since he'd been the one who opened the door to let me into the building, I figured he'd have seen or heard something.

When I entered the barbershop, Sam stood with his back to me, silently staring out the window, focused on something in the parking lot. The smell of soap and hair tonic took me back to when I was a child going to town with Father. Sam had had a little bit of hair on his head back then. Not that a bald barber was unusual, but it had seemed ironic to me and my sisters when we were children.

"Hi, Sam." I spoke quietly so as not to startle him.

When he spun around, an expression of deep sadness covered his features. At the sight of me, his face broke into a smile, and he made his way toward me. "You're still here, Lily?"

"Yes," I said as I took in his new shop.

The walls were covered with plaques, most of which had a funny saying referring to haircuts. I recognized some of them from his place on Main Street and smiled when I found one of my favorites with a pair of scissors and a smiling barber: *Don't just get a haircut, get them all cut.* The room had the same friendly atmosphere that I'd come to associate with Sam as a child. He met me at the counter where someone had placed a stack of free calendars beside the register. The first of the year was still a few months away, but it was coming to the time when businesses gave away New Year's items as an advertisement. Sam's had pictures of kittens and puppies for each new month. On impulse, I took one. Ava would tease me because by the time January first came around, I'd have half a dozen calendars needing a place to be hung. "I had an appointment with Mr. Rinehart."

"Well," Sam said with a serious look on his face. The sad expression was so out of character for the jolly man I'd known as a child. "I'm glad you stopped in to say hi to an old friend. Seeing you here brings back memories of a happier time."

I got the impression he didn't know the accountant was dead, and I didn't know how to break the news to him. After a moment, he started speaking again.

"There seems to be a lot of police activity outside." He nodded in the direction of the parking lot. "Something must be going on upstairs. One of the carpenters hurt himself yesterday and had to be rushed to the hospital. I thought they'd said they were taking today off."

"No, this has nothing to do with the remodeling," I assured him. "I'm sorry to have to tell you that it's because Mr. Rinehart is dead."

Sam's brows, the only facial hair left on his head, creased, and his eyes grew wide with shock. His reaction worried me. The man had to be in his seventies, so I set down my purse and the calendar and raced to his side. "Are you all right?"

"Yes, I'm fine." He waved me away as he took a seat on the tall stool behind his cash register. "Don't worry about me. What happened to Melvin?"

The man's breathing sounded labored to me, and I was worried about him, but he seemed to do better once he sat down.

"I found him on the floor dead when I went in for our appointment," I explained. Since I'd only recently met the accountant, I had no idea if he and the barber were close friends, although I doubted two people so opposite in nature would spend much time together. Sam was friendly and liked to shoot the breeze while Mr. Rinehart had been cold and had worn a perpetual sneer.

"He seemed healthy to me the last time I saw him." Sam sounded confused, but not grievous.

"When was the last time you saw him?" I asked.

"This morning when I came into work." Sam looked at the large Roman numeral clock on the wall. "It must have been around eight."

"I don't think his death had anything to do with his health," I said gently.

After a moment of silence, Sam seemed to get my drift. "You mean someone killed him?"

"Yes, I'm afraid so." Unless that weight fell from a top shelf above him, his death was no accident. "Do you know anyone who would want to see him dead?"

"I don't know for sure." Sam grunted and then rubbed the palm of his hand across the back of his head. "He was a terrible landlord. If you complained about anything, he'd raise the rent."

Why didn't that surprise me? The description fell right into line with my first impression of the man. He wasn't someone I would have wanted to upset or rent property from.

"Was there anyone else in the building when you opened the door for me earlier?" I asked.

"I'm not sure, but I doubt it," Sam said with a shrug. "They don't open the salon on Mondays, but for some reason they didn't open today, either. I didn't see anyone in the lobby. There may have been people upstairs."

"Did you have any customers?" I asked.

"I had a few before lunch." For some reason, he sounded defensive. "The new Family Hair salon in town has taken more than a few of my clientele. People want quick and cheap these days with no sense of loyalty. I miss men like your dad."

"Me too," I whispered. My father would have been in his sixties by now and retired. I wonder why Sam hadn't retired himself. Maybe he couldn't afford to. As I recalled, his wife passed away fifteen years or so ago after a long battle with cancer. That would explain why he'd looked so sad when I first came into the shop. Although he'd seemed spry enough when he let me into the building.

"Where were you headed when I saw you earlier?" I asked.

"I forgot to bring a lunch with me this morning." He gave me a slight grin as if letting me in on a secret. "So, I snuck out to get a bite at the deli down the street."

Suddenly, his demeanor changed, and he raised the palms of his hands. "Hey, I had nothing to do with Melvin's murder."

"I know you well enough to know you would never harm anyone," I assured him. "Are you sure you don't know anyone that would want to kill Mr. Rinehart?"

"Like I said, he's a terrible landlord, or I should say was?" Sam narrowed his eyes, and he stared off into space for a moment before nodding slowly while biting down on the side of his lower lip.

"What is it?" I asked with curiosity filled breath.

"Ethan Pierce rents a building on Main Street from Melvin." Sam tapped the palm of his hand rapidly against the counter, his voice rising with each stroke. "And he's got plenty of reasons to want to see Melvin dead."

"Like what?" I sounded as spellbound as I felt, like a kid hanging on to his every word.

"He's about to lose his ice cream parlor," Sam said, pulling me in with a knowing nod. "And you want to know why? I'll tell you why—because the scrooge wouldn't fix the freezer."

"Oh, that's cold," I said, not intending to make a pun, but it did sound kind of funny. Ava would love the morbid humor when I told her.

CHAPTER THREE
"It takes two to tango."

———

By the time I returned to the office, there were only a few hours left before The Park closed. When I entered the lobby, Gretchen sat behind the large receptionist desk, focused intently on her computer screen. Unaware of my presence, she nibbled on the edge of one of her dark red fingernails as she concentrated on whatever it was that held her interest. I cleared my throat, and she jumped so hard that her chair rolled away from the table.

"I'm back." I gave her a slight wave and wrinkled my nose since I felt guilty for having disturbed her.

The smile on her face faltered when she looked at me. I never had been able to hide my feelings well and as a kid seldom got away with anything. Mother said the emotions on my face read like a book.

"What's wrong?" Gretchen shut down the page she'd had up on the computer and swiveled her chair around to face me better. "Did you see the accountant?"

"No, he's dead." My words came out sounding blunter than I'd wanted.

Gretchen gasped, visibly shaken by my announcement. Her skin paled, and like a fish out of water, her mouth hung open and then closed. She picked up an envelope and fanned the paper in front of her face.

"Are you all right?" I rushed to her side, afraid she'd faint.

"Yes, I'm fine," she said, reaching for the bottled water container she kept on her desk.

She took a sip, and I waited for her to finish taking a drink before I said, "I'm sorry. I didn't realize you knew him."

"We dated once," her voice wobbled, and she blinked away tears in her eyes. "When I first moved to Grady, I didn't know anyone. Melvin was one of the first people to befriend me."

"Oh. Then I am deeply sorry. I had no idea." Flustered, I sounded like a broken record, but I had been out-of-state working as the manager of a park in the Ozarks back when Gretchen moved to Grady. In her late forties, she had wanted to get out of the city and tried to open an accounting office in our small community, but due to lack of interest, she had to close. When The Park's planning committee offered her a position here, she jumped at the opportunity.

"Our relationship didn't last long," she explained. "Back then, I'd been wrapped up in trying to start my business, and he was well established. We had so much in common, and he'd been so persistent. Looking back, I realize he was just sizing up the competition, which was fine since he really wasn't my type."

The two of them, as a couple, didn't fit. Even though I hardly knew the man, from what I had witnessed, he was dull, snooty, and egotistical. Gretchen, on the other hand, was friendly, vibrant, and full of life.

"It's been ages since we've even spoken to one another," she said. "It was kind of awkward when he came by with Steve."

"I understand," I said, although there had been no sign of recognition between the two of them when Melvin had been here yesterday. It was hard for me to believe that it had been a little more than twenty-four hours ago. Regardless, she looked upset now. "Why don't you clock out early?"

"As much as I hate to, going home right now sounds like a good idea." She gathered her things and shut down the computer.

"Are you sure you'll be all right?" I asked with concern. "Maybe you shouldn't be alone."

"But I won't be." A heartfelt smile spread across her face. "With everything that's been going on, I haven't had a chance to tell you that my brother Robert came to visit last night. It was a surprise."

"Good," I said. Gretchen had one sibling, a younger brother who she often spoke of with great pride. "I'm glad you won't be alone. Call me if you need to talk."

"Thanks, Lily." Her eyes filled with tears. "I'll see you in the morning."

I gave her a hug before she left. In my office, I sat down and took a deep breath and then logged onto my computer. As I scrolled through my messages, I realized Gretchen never asked how Melvin died. Odd as it seemed, the shock of his death had clearly sent her for a loop.

Half an hour before closing time, the front door chimed, but before I could get out of my office, I heard Ava call from the lobby, "It's just me."

I opened my door wide enough to stick my head out. "Come on back."

Ava came to visit me, bearing leftover brownies and two small cartons of milk she must have picked up at the café. She placed the items on the desk and then dragged one of the spare chairs around to my side of the desk and took a seat.

Before I had time to thank her for the unexpected treat, a look of concern washed over her face. "Are you okay?"

"Yes. I'm fine." I pinched off a corner of the brownie she'd placed in front of me and plopped the yummy morsel into my mouth. The sweet sensation of chewy chocolate goodness teased my taste buds and filled me with happy vibes. I raised the carton of milk to my lips and took a sip.

"How did the meeting with the accountant go?" Ava's question brought me back down to earth.

I let out a gulp, swallowed too fast, and coughed, but thankfully managed not to spit anything out of my mouth. Ava patted my back and handed me a napkin. It took a moment for me to regain my composure. I'd forgotten she didn't know about Melvin Rinehart. My third dead body in less than a year seemed to have dulled my senses and given me emotional callousness. Ava was going to come unglued when she realized the murder had happened not so long ago.

"He was dead when I got there," I said. By the look on her face, you'd have thought I'd suddenly grown a third arm.

"Why—are you . . .? What did you just say?" she stuttered.

"Honest." I had to blink away the moisture from my eyes from having coughed so hard. "Someone killed him before I got there."

"You mean." My sister let out a sharp gasp, and her eyes widened with surprise. "You were the one who found his body?"

I simply nodded. Ava looked so dumbfounded that I immediately regretted having spoken so frankly. She didn't say a word for several minutes. I was about to ask if she was all right when she finally spoke. "What did you do?"

"I called Jack," I said with a shrug. "There wasn't much else I could do. By the time I'd discovered Mr. Rinehart, it was too late for EMTs to help him."

She took a deep breath and blew it out before saying, "Why don't you start from the beginning and tell me everything?"

After I'd filled her in on my afternoon in town, I recalled the buckwheat coin I'd picked up from the sidewalk. I had to dig around in my purse to find it. "While I was there, I found something to add to your collection."

What's that?" she asked.

"A penny." I held the coin up for my sister to see.

"Oh." Her eyes lit with delight. "Find a penny, pick it up, and all day long, you'll have good luck!"

Ava took it from me and squinted. She flipped it over and wrinkled her nose. "This is not a penny. It's too little, and it looks more like a cufflink from some kind of uniform."

"Are you kidding?" I took the circular object from her to take a closer look. She was correct. The disc was smaller than a penny and more the size of a dime. Apparently, I needed to have my vision checked.

Ava peered over my shoulder, watching with her eagle eyes, waiting for my assessment.

"Wow, you're right," I admitted, feeling a little silly for thinking I'd found something of value.

"Am I ever not?" Ava asked playfully.

I ignored my sister and continued to examine the object. There was a design only on one side. The reverse surface was flat and smooth, with a little knot where a hook had once been. What appeared to be a logo of some sort had a name encircled by a wreath. "The Cloverleaf." I read aloud and looked at Ava. "I've never heard of it."

"Me either," Ava said eagerly, always ready to solve a mystery. "Let's Google it,"

I entered the name on my computer, and we both peered at the screen, waiting for The Park's less than stellar internet service to do its thing. The top finds were a lake in Wisconsin, a city in Texas, and a tavern in New Jersey. None of them had logos that looked anything like the design we were looking for.

"Try looking up the word, 'cloverleaf,' without 'the'" Ava suggested.

When I did, I got a pizza restaurant and a paper company in Ohio. Nothing close to what we were searching for came up, so I dropped the mystery object back into my purse, even though it would most likely end up in the trash. For now, I wanted to hang on to it until I got home and could use our high-speed Wi-Fi to find out more about the mysterious markings.

"So." Ava shot me a piercing stare and changed the subject. "Who do you think killed the accountant, and why?"

"I don't know," I said. "The only other person I saw in the building at the time was Sam Smith."

"Dad's old barber?" Ava let out a low whistle. "I can't remember the last time I saw Sam. It's been years. Did he remember you?"

"Yes, I talked to him before I left the building," I said. "When I pressed him for information, he suggested Ethan Pierce, who runs the ice cream parlor on Main Street, may have had something to do with the murder."

"Wait, let me see if I have this right. The barber thinks the ice cream man killed the accountant?" Her expression was as silly as the words she'd strung together in satire.

"In the den with the paperweight," I added, reminded of the children's board game we'd played when we were young.

"Do you really think Ethan did it?" she asked in all seriousness.

"No, or at least, I don't know if he did," I answered quickly. "I haven't spoken with him yet."

"Why would Ethan want to kill Mr. Rinehart?" Ava asked. "I can understand being upset if he messed up his tax return or something, but not bad enough to kill."

"Ethan rents a building space from Melvin on Main Street, and according to Sam, Mr. Rinehart wasn't much of a landlord," I told her. "The ice cream freezer isn't working, and it's cutting into his profits."

A sly smile spread across her face. "It sounds like we need to do some early Christmas shopping in downtown Grady on the way home."

"That sounds like a great idea to me." I shut down my computer while Ava cleaned up our mess from the brownies and milk. "And get some ice cream while we're there."

"Wait." Ava slid her chair back against the wall where it belonged and glanced at me. "I thought his ice cream machine didn't work."

"The long display freezer is on the blink." I picked up my purse and stood. "But we can still buy soft serve or shakes that come out of the soft serve machine."

"I guess that means they only have vanilla or chocolate to choose from," Ava said as we left my office. "That would be hard on his business."

"Yes, limiting choices to just two would certainly take a bite out of sales," I agreed. Last summer, we went in there while out shopping on Main Street, and there were at least a dozen different flavors of ice cream to choose from.

I parked the jeep on Main Street half a block from the ice cream parlor. Grady was a quaint little town, rich in history. Shop owners packed the antique stores with unique Old West items for early Christmas shoppers. The leather shop displayed custom-made belts and holsters decorated with handstamped patterns such as lovely floral designs and oak leaf clusters. Sweet sugary smells permeated the air outside the Old Timey Candy Shop. The two-story antique emporium had a row of lanterns in its front window. Ava had a spring in her steps. She loved buying Christmas gifts. As for myself, I was a last-minute shopper, but Ava liked to get her shopping done before Thanksgiving. The weather was perfect for taking a stroll. A local band played in the pocket park on the corner.

We didn't want to appear too obvious, so we sauntered along the sidewalk looking at the window displays. When we stepped inside Ethan's Ice Cream Parlor, there were three teenage girls at the counter paying for their drinks. We waited for them to leave before we moved up to place our orders. I ordered a chocolate shake, and Ava wanted vanilla.

"It's kind of quiet around here tonight," I said to the man taking our order as Ava counted out money to pay for our ice cream. "Are you the owner?"

"Yeah, it's been that way for a while now," Ethan mumbled. He was a big man, at least six feet tall, with a muscular build. Tattoos covered his neck and arms, and he wore a black and white bandanna around his head. Not your typical ice cream man.

"Do you have any idea why?" I asked innocently and glanced out the large front window. "There seem to be a lot of people out shopping."

He grunted and jabbed his thumb in the cooler's direction. Instead of rows of buckets filled with flavors to choose from, there were four handwritten signs spaced across the glass partition. "No scooped ice cream, shakes half price."

"I haven't been able to sell hand scooped ice cream for over a week." His nostrils flared. "The health department shut down everything but the shake machine because of a drainage issue and the freezer being on the blitz."

"Oh, my." I played dumb. "You'd think the landlord would help you with that."

"The old crook has been dragging his feet about getting the freezer fixed." Ethan picked up a cloth and started wiping down the counters. From the sound of it, he didn't know Melvin was dead, or if he did, he was an excellent actor.

"Were you open this morning?" I asked before taking a long sip of the thick chocolate sweetness through the straw.

"No, I was at home alone, going through the help wanted ads." He tossed the white cloth over his shoulder and pushed various buttons on the side of the shake dispenser as he spoke. "I have to pay child support, so I'm looking for a part-time job."

"What time did you open today?" I asked, finding it odd he felt the need to tell me he was by himself earlier in the day. Did he have something to hide? Child support suggested he was divorced or separated.

He paused, swiveled to face our direction, and waved his pointer finger at me as if something had suddenly occurred to him. "Were you two looking to buy ice cream earlier today?"

"No, I just wanted to give my family an idea of when they can bring the kids by for some ice cream." If my hands hadn't been full, I would have crossed my fingers even though what I'd said wasn't a complete lie. The twins liked to eat ice cream. "This shake is good, and at half price it's a great deal."

"I didn't open this morning until twelve thirty," he finally admitted with a look of guilt.

"That's a reasonable hour." Ava gave him an encouraging smile. "Most people don't eat ice cream before noon."

I mentally calculated the probable hours of the accountant's death and Ethan's self-confessed schedule. He'd had more than enough time to hit the accountant over the head and then open the ice cream parlor by half-past twelve.

"I guess you haven't heard that Melvin Rinehart is dead," I said, wanting to gauge his response to the news.

He looked startled for a moment and then said, "Oh well, maybe things will improve now that Brynn will own the place."

"Brynn?" I didn't know who he was talking about, but she must be a partner or relative of the accountant's to be taking over the business. "Who is she?'

"She's the old man's niece. Brynn was his only living relative," he explained as the bell above the door dinged to announce a new customer. "He planned to leave everything to her."

"How do you know that?" I asked since there couldn't have been time for a reading of the will yet.

"It's why she moved out here," Ethan said. "He wanted her to take over for him one day."

And therefore, making her the person with the most to gain from the man's death.

CHAPTER FOUR

"There's no use crying over spilled milk."

———

The next day, when I walked into the office, the first thing I noticed was Gretchen had on a new outfit. As The Park's resident fashionista, the woman had great taste in clothes. Everything she wore was vibrant with cheerful colors. Like sunshine on the horizon, she had a way about her that brightened a room, drawing all eyes to her. This new ensemble included an ocean-blue pleated midi skirt with a matching blouse and a necklace on a long chain. Tall and thin, she could have been a model. I needed to ask her to take me shopping with her one day.

"I love your outfit," I told her after I'd put away my things and returned to the lobby. "Is it new?"

"Thanks, and yes, it is." She stood and spun around with her arms out before sitting back down. It looked like she'd made a full recovery from the news about her ex-boyfriend's murder. In fact, she seemed more bubbly than normal.

"Any special occasion?" I asked. Her birthday wasn't until April, and I didn't think she was seeing anyone.

"I have a lunch date with my brother today," she said, scooting her chair closer to the desk. "I don't get to see him very often."

"Oh, that's right. You told me he was in town. His name is Robert, isn't it?" I had an excellent memory, and as manager, I'd reviewed all the employees' records. "I don't think I've met him yet."

She swiveled her chair around until she faced her computer. "You missed him last time he was here. Back in September, when we went on that retreat, we stopped by so you could meet him, but they said you had back-to-back tours."

"Right, I remember. Joyce said the two of you had been by." The Park's busiest time is late summer and early fall. "Did you have a nice visit last night?"

"Yes. Robert's ten years younger than me and has a great job that keeps him moving," she said with pride in her voice and then grinned. "He hates it when I call him my baby brother. But it's an older sister's job to bug her siblings."

"Well, I hope I'll get to meet him this time." I lightly tapped my fingers against the top of her PC and then proceeded toward what my sisters and I playfully referred to as the administrative center in the back of the building.

"You know where to find me if you need me," I called out when I reached my office door.

Alone in my tiny room, I took a seat behind the desk and turned on my computer. From outside the window, I heard sounds of The Park coming to life. Eager footsteps pounded on the boardwalk. Children called out in excitement, urging their parents to hurry. The chatter would increase as more guests arrived throughout the day.

I pulled my thoughts from the activity outside and rolled my chair closer to the desk. First things first, I liked to start the day reading my emails. The posts from The Park's website came to my work email address along with inner office correspondences. The first one came from someone wanting to know if we rented out The Park for birthday parties. They must not realize how big we were. The ghost town had once been alive, a thriving community with families, business owners, and prospectors. In my reply, I explained that although we did not rent out the entire complex, we would rent out a particular facility, such as the saloon or the restaurants, for a certain amount of time.

The next post came from someone who claimed to have lost money at The Park and asked that we contact them if we should find a one-hundred-dollar bill. I responded, letting them know we would be sure to advise them if their money showed up.

After I'd finished updating the page, I added upcoming events we had planned for The Park, and then moved to my office email. One of them, sent by the chairman of the board, had been flagged as urgent. My heart froze. What bad news did Steve have for me now? With dread and curiosity, I started reading. The planning committee had put a hold on all proposed improvements until they could hire a new auditor. Per Steve, new information provided by Melvin before his death needed to be reviewed before they allocated more funds.

My phone rang, and the caller ID showed Gretchen's name. As my assistant, she would have also received a copy of the email. "Did you see the message from the boss?" When it was only the two of us, she referred to Steve as the boss.

"Yes, I did." I kept my voice soft and steady to counter any concerns brewing in her mind.

"It sounds ominous to me," she said in a whisper, even though, as far as I knew, we were the only two in the building.

"There's nothing to worry about," I assured her. "They're just taking precautions by following company protocol."

Gretchen let out a relieved sigh. "Good. Do you think this hold on expenses will affect the petty cash account for the office?"

"No," I said since she had a justifiable concern. "You'll still have access to funds to buy supplies for The Park."

"That's good," she said and then cleared her throat. "We're expecting a delivery of ink for the copier and new air filters for the office today."

"Don't worry." I kept my voice light, although I had no idea what to expect in the coming days. "It sounds like the committee wants to wait before making any new major changes. Everything else will run as normal."

At least, I hoped I was right. Next, I went over the rest of my emails and found a few inquiries from different employees regarding upcoming events. After I'd replied to all of them, there was a stack of paperwork I'd been putting off that needed to be done. By the time I'd finished, it was close to lunchtime. The chef's salad and a Diet Coke I'd brought from home were in the mini fridge out in the employee kitchen. When I stepped into the lobby, I noticed Gretchen looking at the chain around her neck. A white gold-blue sapphire infinity swirl pendant with diamonds shimmered under the bright lights.

"Oh, how pretty," I said and reached out my hand. "Can I see?"

"Thanks." She pulled the necklace away from her body to give me a closer look. "It was a gift."

Tiny but beautiful, I hadn't noticed the stone earlier. For the second time in less than a week, it occurred to me I needed to book an appointment with the eye doctor. First, I'd mistaken a cuff link for a penny, and this morning I'd totally missed this necklace.

"That reminds me. I found something the other day, but I'm not sure where it came from." I dug in my purse for the object I'd mistaken for a wheat back penny. "Maybe you'll know."

I had the cufflink in my hand ready to show her, when a man I'd never seen before entered the lobby. He wore his hair slicked back and smelled of clay pomade. The short, boxed beard and charming smile brought to my mind a picture of a boyish-looking Ryan Reynolds, but that's where all resemblances ended.

"Hi Robert," Joy and pride filled Gretchen's eyes when she turned her face to include me. "Lily, this is my brother I told you about."

I let the cufflink fall into my purse and reached out to shake Robert's hand.

"Hello, it's nice to meet you," he said and gave me a firm handshake. "My sister has told me a lot about you."

I wondered what his sister had said about me. Not much taller than me with an athletic build, Robert was blond like Gretchen. Only his eyes were dark brown, sat close together above high cheekbones. Overall, he seemed nice, if not a little nervous.

"We're going out for lunch," Gretchen announced as she shut off her computer and pushed her chair away from the desk. "But I'll be back in an hour."

"Take your time," I said. "It's not every day you get to see your brother."

"Thanks." She grabbed her purse, and the two of them headed for the door.

After they were gone, I retrieved my lunch from the kitchen fridge and returned to my office, ready to do a little investigating during my break. I'd forgotten about wanting to research the markings on the cufflink until I was at breakfast this morning, so I brought my high-speed wireless box to work with me. Between bites, I looked up the symbol on the cufflink again. This time I spent more time investigating and found the image was a logo to a casino in Lake Tahoe. The cufflink must have come from a uniform worn by an employee of The Cloverleaf. How in the world did it end up down here?

I'd finished the last swig of my Diet Coke when my walkie talkie went off.

"Sheriff Tom." Tall and thin, the actor playing the town sheriff was one of the ghost town's most liked players. "Calling Miss Cranston. Come in, Miss Cranston."

Even though walkie talkies hadn't been invented until fifty years after the founding of Calico Rock, they were our primary form of communication. The owners of The Park forbid anything more modern to be used by the employees while on duty.

"Yes. This is Miss Cranston," I answered politely, as we'd trained our employees to do when guests were within hearing distance of our conversations. "Sheriff Tom, what can I do for you?"

"We have a group of cowpokes here who'd like to take a tour of our fine city. Why don't you mosey on down here and meet them if you have the time?"

The ticket office for group tours was outside the sheriff's office, and over time, the lawman had become the person responsible for arranging impromptu tours. Most of our guests scheduled their tours ahead of time, but occasionally, a group asked for a special viewing.

"Of course," I said, putting a smile in my voice for the guests. "I'll be right there."

One of the more interesting aspects of my job was meeting people from all around the world. There were ten people standing in front of the jailhouse when I arrived. Most tours averaged between five and twelve people, so this was an average sized group. So far, the smallest I'd had was two and the largest twenty. Ten was a good number to work with.

"Howdy," I said after adjusting my bonnet. "My name's Lily, and I'm happy to show you around Calico Rock. Only be sure to watch for ghosts as we near the mine."

Our standard introduction referred to reports of ghost sightings near the entrance of the mine by several people over the years. I'd never seen anything spooky myself, but a few people claimed to have seen a ghost they believed was the spirit of the town's founder, Thomas Grady, while others believed the phantom was the apparition of a Native American chief guarding the gold. Either way, the intro needed tweaking after the whole fiasco we'd had last summer, but I hadn't gotten around to thinking up a new script yet.

"Where are you folks from?" I asked, keeping my voice and facial expressions folksy and friendly.

There were four women and six men, all upwards of sixty-five except one who I guessed to be about twenty-five. They did not appear to be a family group.

"From different parts of the states," a short stout gray-haired woman with glasses informed me and then added, "I'm Jillian, and we all met online, except for my granddaughter here, Chelsea." The woman wrapped an arm around the only one among them that looked younger than fifty-five. "Her folks sent her along to make sure I stayed out of trouble. We call ourselves Fans of the Old West."

I liked Jillian. She was friendly, sassy, and apparently the speaker for the group. Our first stop was the Old Timey Candy Shop across the road. As we made our way along the boardwalk, visiting different stations, I shared stories about Thomas Grady and his family. Everyone in the group was over twenty-one, so we went into the saloon for a drink. As we sat waiting for the drinks we'd ordered (mine was a sweet tea since I was on the clock), the group grew quiet, so I asked, "Would you like to hear the story about the time a cat saved Thomas Grady from being bitten by a rattlesnake?"

"Please, do tell." Jillian's friends nodded along with her.

"One day," I said, reciting the familiar tale, "while headed out to check on the crew working the mine, Mr. Grady came across one of the stray cats living on the property. This one in particular had been one of his favorites, as she was a friendly black and white tuxedo cat and would let them pet her. They called her Bug for reasons unknown to us today."

"That is a strange name for a cat," Chelsea said just as the drinks arrived.

I waited until we were all settled again before I continued, "Anyhow, Bug had been staring at something on the ground and didn't acknowledge Mr. Grady as he drew near, which was highly unusual. He noticed something in the grass had the feline's full attention. It turned out to be a rattler. Mr. Grady pulled his gun but hesitated when he realized the snake wasn't moving. He figured the reptile must have been dead but kept his weapon drawn just in case. On closer inspection, he learned the snake was alive but was in the process of digesting a mouse. He credits Bug for saving his life because if the snake hadn't upset the cat by stealing its dinner, the creature would have been slithering right in his path."

"I noticed a stray cat near the parking lot," one of the quieter members of the group said before she took a sip from her glass.

"Yes, we have a few around here," I said, careful not to mention Casper by name. The Park's favorite stray that hung out in the cemetery was shy and sending a herd of eager tourists searching for the friendly ghost cat would be an invasion of privacy. "Who knows, one may very well be a descendant of Bug."

When I got back to the office, I discovered Gretchen had returned from her lunch date while I had been away. Facing the computer, she had her back to me when I entered the lobby. To get her attention, I cleared my throat. She glanced in my direction and gave me a quick smile before turning her attention to the monitor.

"How did lunch go?" I asked.

"Oh, we had a pleasant time." Gretchen raised her face, and then she smiled, but her eyes were red and puffy.

"Are you sure?" She didn't look like someone who'd returned from a pleasant visit with their closest relative.

"Yes, don't mind me." She gave me an embarrassed wave of the hand. "I just hate that he can't stay longer. He's so much younger than me, and I practically raised him since both of our parents worked full-time jobs. Robert owns a special part of my heart."

"Will he be leaving so soon?" From what she had told me, I got the impression he'd only recently showed up.

"He's not sure," she said with a sniffle. "But it could be any time. How long he gets to stay depends on when they call him back."

"That's a shame," I said with compassion. She was upset, and I understood since I hated to be separated from my sisters as well. "Where does he work?"

"He does seasonal jobs for county owned golf courses in the Southwest." She snagged a Kleenex from the box beside her pen holder. "So, he moves around a lot."

"Well, if you need anything, just let me know." My words were heartfelt, too. Gretchen was a vital part of our team, and one thing we valued at The Park was family.

CHAPTER FIVE

"All is fair in love and war."

———

Fridays were one of my busiest days at work. During the morning hours, actors prepared for the shootout on Main Street, which took place in front of the Sheriff's office across from the saloon and the bank. In the past, we'd held the popular event on Saturday and Sunday, but with growth in attendance, the planning committee had set up an online survey to get a feel for the guests' preferences and the overwhelming results showed they preferred Fridays over Sundays. Even after adjusting the days, the event still drew a crowd of loyal western fans. As I walked along Main Street, I recognized the members from yesterday's tour group among the swarm of people.

Employees dressed in character costumes were easy to spot. It did my heart good to see the number of guests well outnumbered the staff. The opposite had been true a few months ago, but now Grady's little ghost town was alive and well. Out of nowhere, a hand came to rest on my back. I twisted my head to look up into Cody's dark brown eyes. I felt my heart leap, and on their own accord, the edges of my lips stretched upward.

"Are you ready for the show?" The warmth in his eyes intensified.

"Now I am," I said with a grin, surprised at myself for flirting so blatantly.

Local law officers took turns volunteering to keep the shows safe. Actors from Placerville came in and had specialized equipment for what was more or less a live action play. As the highest-ranking employee on sight during the show, it was my job to stay close to the officer on duty in case anything happened. Although I'd seen Cody's name on the schedule for this morning, I'd assumed he'd have another officer take his place since he was in the middle of a murder investigation.

"I'm surprised you're able to be here today." Hopefully, my cheeks didn't look as warm as they suddenly felt. "Because, for some reason, I thought you'd be busy elsewhere."

Cody glanced around before he leaned in closer. The woodsy scent of his cologne mingling with peppermint candy on his breath drew my attention away from the proceedings. His warm breath on my cheek made it hard for me to concentrate on anything other than the handsome man beside me. "Parker's running late, and since I was in the area, I told him I'd stand by until he could get here."

"In the area," I said in surprise. Located outside of town, there weren't other businesses or homes *in the area* of The Park.

"Just doing a follow up." He gave me a vague reply before adding, "Apparently Mr. Rinehart had been getting death threats for years from disgruntled clients."

For some reason, that statement didn't surprise me, although it should have. Murder was never the answer. I lowered my voice and gazed into his eyes. "So, do you have any leads on who killed him?"

"Officer West," Nick, a member of the stunt crew, jogged up to where we stood. "We're ready to have the weapons inspected."

Cody reached out and squeezed my hand before leaving. "We'll talk more later."

The two men marched off toward the trailer where the team kept their equipment. They used fake weapons, but each one had to be looked over by an officer before being fired. On my own again, I visited with guests on the boardwalk while we waited for the action to start. It never failed to amaze me how so many people traveled great distances to enjoy our establishment. The locals and loyal attenders mingled along with the out of towners. A while later, when the time came for the show to start, it was Parker Sloan and not Cody who stepped out from the maintenance office. I recognized the shorter man's athletic build when he took his place beside the stuntmen's supply cart. Head of the maintenance department, he wore his reserve deputy uniform, prepared to watch over the proceedings. Cody must have gone back to work, but I'd be sure to speak with him later. I wanted to know all about those threats he'd mentioned earlier.

"Someone, stop them!" John Porter ran out onto the street, waving his hands in the air. Tall, thin, and dressed in a three-piece suit, as you'd expect a banker from the Wild West, he was one of our best reenactors. "They just robbed the bank."

The only brick building in town, wrought iron bars covered the glass windows and door of the Grady Town Bank. From the alleyway beside the building, three cowboys on horseback came riding onto Main Street with guns drawn, firing into the air. They carried bags of money strapped to the saddles as they headed in the direction of the mine.

Sheriff Tom ran out of his office across the road. He stood in the middle of the street and fired toward the outlaws, but they rode off without any of them being hit.

"I need a posse of men who can shoot, ride, and aren't afraid to die," he shouted as he jumped on a white horse tied to the hitching post in front of the jailhouse.

Moments later, a group of five men on tall horses wearing chaps, Stetsons, and belts loaded with ammo rode up to join him. They all followed the lawman headed out of town after the bank robbers. Gone from our view, time seemed to slow and soon the crowd of onlookers started to chatter and mingle until Rodney Reich, the town's brawny blacksmith, came jogging into town from the direction the riders had all gone. "The posse's coming back. They've got two of them rascally critters with them."

Riding in much slower than they left, the good guys rode back in with two glum looking bad guys with their hands bound. With the help of his men, Sheriff Tom dragged the outlaws into the jailhouse. After his helpers left the building, the lawman stepped out onto the covered porch and took a seat in his rocker, looking mighty proud.

"What happened to the third one, Sheriff?" someone from the crowd called.

It was hard to tell if the question came from an actor or a guest. We'd trained the reenactors to handle just about anything thrown their way.

"More than likely, he's laid out at the bottom of a gully somewhere." Tom crossed his arms and smiled.

"Sheriff." Trudy, one of the girls from the saloon, with feathers in her hair and a noticeably short red dress, came strolling up the walkway. "The Clayton brothers are at it again, and Max needs your help at the saloon."

"Dag-nab-it," Tom spit chewing tobacco out of the side of his mouth and stood. "When will those boys ever learn to behave themselves in public?"

The sheriff and Trudy walked away from the jail and disappeared into the saloon across the street. The crowd grew quiet, as if they weren't sure if the show was over or not. This time there wasn't any curious chatter as the spectators looked left and right for signs of activity.

Suddenly, the third bank robber came sneaking out from behind the jailhouse. Guns drawn and raised high, he kept his back pressed against the side of the building as he crept to the front porch, looked both ways to make sure the coast was clear, and then slipped inside.

Ava came to stand beside me. "Which one is it?"

She must have walked down from the schoolhouse to watch the show.

"The jail break," I whispered, not wanting to give anything away to anyone nearby who may be new to the experience.

The stunt team actors had several scripts they followed. I'd seen all of them more than a few times, but still they never felt old, as they changed them enough for each one to feel like a new show.

By himself now, Sheriff Tom returned from the saloon whistling as he neared his office. He stepped onto the porch, walked to the door, and stood still. A hush fell over the audience as the Sheriff tilted his head upward as if something didn't feel right. You could have heard a pebble fall onto the gravel road as the lawman reached for the door handle. He went inside the building, and the sound of gunfire started until silence fell once again.

"Sheriff?" one of his deputies slipped out from his hiding place behind the livery stable and crept toward the jail.

Suddenly the door flew open, and after a moment, Sheriff Tom stumbled onto the porch, bleeding. "Someone, get me a doctor," he yelled.

"You okay, Sheriff?" asked the deputy.

"Yeah." The lawman clutched his bloodied arm and leaned against the doorpost. "But those no accounts inside need a doctor."

The crowd applauded, and the actors came out to take their bows.

"Aww." Ava sighed while clapping her hands. "It wasn't the one with the girl outlaw. I love that one."

"Me too," I agreed. The script with the innocent outlaw rescued by the sheriff had more of a romantic twist. "Maybe next time."

"I wanted to let you know I'm going out to eat with a friend, so I won't need a ride home tonight." Ava's face flushed with a healthy hue.

The smile on her face added to my suspicion that my little sister had a date. If so, I felt glad for her. If anyone deserved to be happy, it was Ava. Her husband had died many years ago, less than two years after they'd married.

"Who with?" I asked as I placed my hand on her arm. She had to have known I wouldn't let her get off without more information.

She shook her head, grinning playfully, refusing to answer my question. Ugh, no way was she getting off that easily.

"Do I need to call Pat?" I asked and reached into my pocket as if looking for my cell phone, even though when we were in costume we weren't allowed to carry them.

"Oh, you." She shook her head and sighed as she rolled her eyes. The triple axel. This was serious. "Parker and I are going to grab a bite to eat after work. There's no need to get Pat all excited."

Parker? He was one of the good guys, but I'd never thought of him as dating material for Ava. He had a rocky past but had always been on the level. As the head of the maintenance department, he was one of our most trusted employees as well as a volunteer firefighter and part-time sheriff's deputy. There weren't a lot of men who'd put a child through college when said offspring didn't even know they existed. I'd unintentionally discovered this family secret of his when I was first hired as the director. My snooping had opened a can of worms, but he didn't seem to have held it against me.

"Well, have fun," I said, unable to cover my surprise.

"See you later." Ava stepped away and pivoted in the direction of the schoolhouse and then called out, "Don't wait up for me."

After everything had settled down, I clocked off early because I wanted to pay Brynn a visit. According to Gretchen, Brynn Rinehart was in her late twenties and had moved to Grady a few months ago, after her parents passed away.

Since I didn't feel right about just showing up at a total stranger's house and asking if they killed their uncle, I hoped to find her at the building complex where the accountant had met his demise. I was taking a chance, but if she weren't there, maybe Sam or someone else in the building would be able to give me an idea of how to contact her.

It was midafternoon and sunny out when I pulled the Jeep into the Rinehart Business Complex. To my surprise, the parking lot was full. Two large white crew cab trucks were near the front door, and each one had a set of magnetics advertising Belton and Sons Construction. I recognized Sam's vehicle, but didn't know who the other three cars belonged to. One of them, a red corvette, parked in the space marked as *Owner's Parking* gave me hope the mystery woman would be around.

Inside the building, the sounds of hammers, drills, and the loud voices of the construction workers echoed down from the second floor. Only two days after having found the owner of the establishment's body in his office, there was something almost disrespectful about the activity overhead. But then, as they say, life goes on. Standing at the base of the stairs, I debated if I should go up to the accountant's office or go find Sam and ask him if he knew where I'd find Brynn Rinehart. When I took a step toward the barbershop, a young redheaded woman wearing a stylish black pantsuit with a long black and white mesh duster stepped out from Chloe's beauty salon. I instantly admired her taste in clothing. Tall and curvy, she walked with a purpose, as if she had somewhere else to be. This had to be Brynn. I intercepted her at the entrance. I had to raise my voice to be heard above the noise upstairs. "Excuse me, are you Miss Rinehart?"

"Yes," she said and then glanced at the ceiling. "Let's step outside where we can hear one another."

She pushed the door open and waited for me to exit first. For a moment, I wondered if she was about to prank me and close the door between us. Thankfully, she didn't.

"Hi," I introduced myself once we were both outdoors, "I'm Lily Cranston."

"Nice to meet you. As you guessed, I'm Brynn Rinehart," she said as she brushed wayward strands of her long auburn hair away from her shoulder. "If you're here about the space for rent, I'm afraid it will be a few more weeks until it's ready."

"No, actually I just wanted to stop by to meet you," I said and then quickly explained who I was. "I'm the manager at the Calico Rock Mine and Ghost Town."

"Oh," she said and then paused. Her mouth dropped open, and her eyes widened as if something had suddenly occurred to her. "You must be the one who found my uncle's body."

"Yes," I said softly since I was unsure how she felt about me. Her uncle shouldn't have mentioned me or my supposed criminal actions to her if he were as reputable as he had liked people to believe. "I'm sorry for your loss."

"When the police told me about you, I asked that cute Officer West for your number, but he said he couldn't do that." Cody had never told me anything about Brynn wanting to contact me. Maybe that's what he wanted to talk about. "Let's go out back and sit down by the lake where we can chat."

We crossed over the lawn to the side of the building, where a well-worn path led to a small pond next to a wooded area behind the complex. I had no idea this place was back here. A red picnic table with benches sat underneath an old oak tree. Three ducks were floating on the other side of the water, quacking with excitement when one of them scored a water bug. A short wooden dock painted white stretched out over the water. The view made it easy to understand why she wanted to visit this cozy spot, especially on such a nice day.

"Were you one of Uncle Melvin's clients?" Brynn asked once we'd settled across from each other on the red painted picnic table.

"Not exactly." I pulled my view from the water and looked at her. "He was doing an audit for The Park, and he'd asked me to meet with him at noon the day I found him."

"Oh, wow," she said, sounding sympathetic when, in fact, I was the one who should console her. "That must have been quite a shock for you."

"Yes. It was," I said, and then since she didn't appear to be too upset to talk about him, I asked, "Were you and your uncle close?"

"Not really," she explained, shaking her head briefly. "I grew up in Texas and before moving here, I'd only seen him a few times when he came out to visit my father, who was his brother."

"Oh, I see." That kind of explained her being so upbeat despite the death of her only relative in town.

"When Dad died," she continued, as if we were discussing something as simple as the weather, "Uncle Melvin asked me to move out here and help him with the business. His generous offer surprised me, but since I didn't have any other options, I took him up on the deal."

"How long ago was that?" I wondered how close she had been to her father. If she'd moved here right after his death, his passing had to have been a year or so ago.

"I've been here close to a year now," she explained. "I was Uncle Melvin's only relative, and he wanted to keep his holdings in the family. He was still training me to run the business when someone killed him."

"I'd only met him once, and he seemed highly professional", I told her because it was the only positive description I could think of to describe the man. "Do you have any idea who would have wanted to kill Mr. Rinehart?"

"I haven't met many people other than his renters." With a thoughtful expression on her face, Brynn bit down on the edge of her bottom lip before looking at me. "He didn't seem to have many friends. At home, there's his staff, which consists of a cook and a housecleaner who each come by in the afternoons. In their forties, the two women are cousins, or maybe they're sisters. I forget. They're related somehow, and they seemed happy to be working for Uncle Melvin."

"Do you know if they work somewhere else in the mornings?" If they only worked after noon, either of them could have been the murderer.

"I don't really know," Brynn admitted. "I haven't gotten to know either of them well. They keep to themselves while doing their jobs."

It seemed odd that she'd seen these two women daily for almost a year and knew nothing about them. I pushed aside the brief notion that perhaps Brynn had a hard time getting close to people since she'd been friendly and straightforward with me from the start.

"Oh, it must be different for you, living here in California now," I said.

"I have to admit that it has taken some adjusting," she confessed and then gasped as if reminded of something important. "Oh, there is a neighbor who complains about Uncle Melvin's dogs barking at all hours of the night."

"Do you think they are the type who'd kill someone?" I asked.

From searching online, I knew Mr. Rinehart lived in a gated community near the river, and I wondered what the inside of his home looked like. It had to be big in order to have housed his ego.

"No, not really." Her cheeks dimpled when she scrunched up her mouth and narrowed her eyes. "Besides, they've been out of town for the past two weeks."

"Were you in town the day your uncle died?" I asked.

"Actually, I wasn't." A look of regret crossed her face. "Maybe if I'd been here, he'd still be alive. From eight to twelve, I usually worked in his office. But on Wednesday, I went to the strip malls in Placerville to do some early Christmas shopping."

"By yourself?" I assumed since she'd said she hadn't gotten to know anyone other than their renters, she would have traveled alone.

"Yes." She nodded with a playful grin. "I like to shop by myself. That way I can spend all the time I want looking at the things I'm interested in. Not to sound unsociable, but shopping is a serious business to me."

Brynn glanced at her watch, stood, and grabbed her clutch purse. "Oh, I have to run, or I'll be late for my appointment with the funeral director."

By the time I rose from the bench, she'd already headed for the parking lot. "Let's talk again soon," she called out to me as she sprinted away.

Without Ava around, a cloak of quiet weighed heavy over the house. Not that my sister was a loud person or anything, I simply missed knowing she was within the sound of my voice. Maybe we were growing too stagnant in our daily routine. We were happy living together, or at least, I hope she felt the same way as I did.

My stomach rumbled, reminding me I'd skipped lunch to visit the accountant's niece. I brushed away my useless musings and went into the kitchen. While I waited for the left-over lasagna—from the last time Pat and her family had had dinner with us—to heat in the microwave, I stared at the room around me. The dated light brown oak cabinets could do with a more modern color or stain. The tile floor blended in well, but a new hardwood floor would give the old farmhouse a more modern touch without taking away from its authenticity.

To get away from my nitpicking thoughts, I took my plate into the living room and turned on the television to watch the local news while I ate. As expected, Mr. Rinehart's murder was the top story. There weren't any new leads, and the police were requesting anyone with information to call them. Next came a promise from the news anchor to fill us in on the weather after a short commercial break.

When I'd finished eating, I turned off the tube and filled up the dishwasher instead of listening to more dribble. The house seemed so big and quiet with Ava gone. It had been a while since I'd paid Pat and her family a visit. There was sure to be some sort of activity going on over there.

My phone rang, and I half expected it to be Pat telling me to come over, but Cody's number appeared on the screen. I waited until the second ring to answer. No need to look too eager.

"Hello, stranger!" I said in a playful tone.

"Hey." The warmth in his voice lifted my spirits. "I'm in the area and wondered if you'd care to go for a walk with me."

The mild temperature and cloudless sky would make a lovely night for being outdoors, and walking was a favorite family pastime. On our property, a full-time spring had created a gentle flowing creek that wound through a grove of trees on the west end of the property, and over the years, we'd turned the area into a little walking trail. It had been ages since I'd had time to visit the spot. Besides, I was more than happy to go for a walk with Cody anytime.

"Sure," I said. Hopefully, he'd have news about the investigation to share with me, and I enjoyed spending time with him. "That sounds nice."

"I'll be there in a few minutes." Cody sounded pleased. I heard a car door shut before he added, "I'm just now leaving the mini mart on Second Street."

After we hung up, I hurried upstairs to my room, where I ran a brush through my hair, slipped on my walking shoes, and grabbed a light sweater before bouncing down the stairs. Cocoa looked up from the couch where she'd been napping. The cat gave me a curious look and then let out a wide yawn. I'm not sure why, but I felt nervous waiting for Cody to arrive. At the sound of his cruiser pulling into the driveway, my heart leapt, and my stomach flip-flopped. *Stop acting like a teenager,* I chided myself.

When he knocked on the door, I took a deep breath and stepped outside. He looked great in his suit and tie as he was still working on the case. Otherwise, I'm sure he would have worn something more casual. Maybe I should have left on my pioneer costume. We would have looked like adult trick-or-treaters.

"Sorry I had to run out on you earlier without saying goodbye." He handed me a box of candy. "I hope these will make up for it."

"You didn't have to get me anything. I know you're busy," I told him, but when I looked down, I realized I held a box of chocolate-covered cherries. "Oh, my favorite. How did you know?"

Cody grinned and tapped his pointer finger against his square jaw. "Let's see. We've known each other for at least three decades. I guess somewhere along the way, I picked up on a few of your favorites."

"Oh, really?" I tilted my head to see him better, and feeling up to the challenge, I added, "What's my favorite color?"

"Blue." His answer came fast, and we started walking side by side, headed for the pond.

"That was too easy." I shook my head and laughed since most of my clothes were in various shades of the color. "Anyone with eyes could see I liked blue."

"All right, give me another one." His voice oozed with confidence, and I didn't know if I should feel flattered or irritated.

"What's my favorite season?"

"Fall," he answered quickly.

Hmmm, not bad.

"My favorite animal?"

"Well, I'm pretty sure it's not cows." He eyed the old red barn once used to milk the dairy cattle on Dad's farm. The smell and noise were two things I did not miss. Cody raised his shoulders from side to side, as if searching for an answer while his eyes danced with laughter.

"Could it possibly be cats?" he asked, while holding the outdoor swing for me to take a seat.

"Yes, you are correct," I said, and he sat down beside me. I wanted to change the subject. There were more important things to discuss. Although I knew he couldn't or wouldn't come right out and tell me, I still took a chance and asked, "Any leads?"

"Nothing solid." Was his tactful response. Cody must have seen the expression of doubt on my face, but instead of giving me details, he pushed his foot against the ground and set our swing into motion. "Just following up on a few things."

"I'm surprised one of your follow-ups took you so close to The Park," I said. He had to know I wouldn't give up that easily. "Especially down Old Quarry Road. There's nothing out that way that I can think of."

Cody gave me a funny look and then a smile lit his face. "They put in a trailer park while you were living out of state."

"Oh, my sisters never mentioned it to me," I said with raised brows, and then to see what his response would be, I added, "I'll have to check it out sometime."

"You should," he said with a nod, which told me his lead had been a dead-end. "It's down by the river. A bunch of retired folks live out there enjoying fishing and living away from town."

Like a teenager on a first date, Cody stretched his hands over his head and then placed his right arm on the back of the seat behind me and looked up at the stars. Holding back a giggle, I leaned my head against his forearm and glanced upward. "Were any of them clients of the accountant?"

Cody leaned closer and whispered as if passing on highly classified information, "Rinehart had clients all over the county."

"Surely they didn't all want to kill him." I sat straight, ready to press for more, but the sight of his strong profile and handsome grin stopped me short. If Pat could see me now, she'd shake her head in disbelief and say, "*You're blowing it, Lily.*"

"I can't say for sure." He looked thoughtful as he kept his gaze on the heavens. "But we have had to check on a few."

Finally catching on, I laid my head back and felt his muscular biceps flex. "Anyone I might know?"

"Not likely." He slowed the swing's movement with his foot and turned his face to me. "There's no need for you to get involved in this case. No one you know is under suspicion."

"I'm aware of that." I raised the box of chocolates in my hand, tracing the edges of the black and gold cardboard container with my fingers. "But I can't help feeling that if I knew who killed the accountant, it would help me understand who is trying to frame me."

I stilled my hands and looked over at him. "Do you have any leads on that case?"

"Nope." He shook his head. "Since The Park owners have not reported a crime, there's nothing for us to do."

"Except wait." I sighed and wondered what would happen if they waited too long. "I didn't take any money."

"I know you didn't." He gently removed his arm from behind me and took my hand in his. Cody rubbed his thumb across my wrist for a moment before he cleared his throat. My heart seemed to stall in my chest. The way he looked at me, there was something in his eyes besides the normal warmth that was always there. This was more like a deep longing that took my breath away.

I raised my hand to touch his face when the rush of an engine revving, followed by a set of truck lights, came up the long drive as a vehicle pulled into the driveway. Cody rose from the swing. He kept his focus on the truck but looked surprised at our having another visitor so late.

"Ava had a date tonight," I explained as I tucked the candy into the pocket of my sweater.

"Really?" he cocked his head to the side and crossed his arms.

"Yes," I said, surprised to see him take on Jack's protective brother stance. To ease his mind, I placed my hand on his arm and quickly added, "With Parker."

"Aww." A pleased smile played across his lips.

I trusted Cody's judgment, and if Parker had his approval, then I was good with him dating my sister. Pat and Jack would be the final hurdle, but since Jack hired Parker to serve as a reserve deputy, he had to be sharp. I only worried since my sister hadn't dated anyone in years, and I didn't even know she and Parker had been getting close. Now that Parker's estranged daughter, who he'd been secretly putting through college, had graduated, I guess he had time and money to enjoy life.

Cody and I continued toward the house but slowed our steps as if in agreement to give them privacy.

"Remember when we met back in high school?" His question surprised me.

He had been a sophomore when I was a freshman. New in town, his good looks and friendly personality got him a lot of attention, especially from the girls.

He took my hand, and we stopped walking.

"Yes, I remember," I said, thankful the shadows hid my warm cheeks.

"I never told you this." The honesty in his voice caught my interest. Not that he didn't already have it, but even more so now I wanted to hear what he had to say. "But I had a crush on you back then."

He had to be kidding. The cutest boy in school, he could have dated anyone he wanted to. In fact, he had. By his senior year he and my friend, Tracy, were the most popular dating couple on campus. "Why didn't you ever ask me out then?"

He grinned and said, "I was too intimidated."

I let out a gasp of surprise. "By me?"

Nerdy, emotional, troublemaker, those were all words that would have fit me as a teenager, but not intimidating.

"Yes and no." He let out a short laugh, took my hand, and we continued walking as he explained. "The Cranston sisters were a force in high school. Your parents were important people in the community, and the three of you girls were popular and so close."

By the time we reached the porch, Parker had left, and Ava was inside the house. Cody placed his hand on my arm and pulled me around to face him. "Thanks," he said.

I looked up into his dark brown eyes filled with an intense emotion and suddenly realized the temperature had grown unseasonably warm for this time of year. "What for?"

"For going for a walk with me." Cody placed his right hand on my cheek and then brushed my hair back. I started to say something, but before I could, he ducked his head and pressed his lips against mine. His kiss was warm and gentle. On impulse, I reached out my arms and wrapped them around his neck. He pulled me closer, and our embrace deepened.

"Lily?" Ava called out from inside the house, and Cody broke our kiss, leaving both of us breathless.

"Good night." Cody gazed deep into my eyes and tingles warmed my skin. He opened the door for me and then stepped back.

"Good night." I wiggled the fingers on my free hand and slipped inside without breaking eye contact with him until the door shut.

"Oh, did I wake you?" Ava came out from the kitchen by the time I'd reached the bottom of the stairs. In her hands, she held two bowls of freshly popped popcorn. Without waiting for me to answer, she looked at my clothes. "No, I guess not. Were you out for a walk?"

"Yes," I answered without giving her any details.

"Alone?" she asked, knowing full well I didn't like being out in the dark by myself anymore, since I'd had an awful experience last summer while out alone at night.

"Cody just left." When I said his name, my voice sounded airy and whimsical.

Ava smiled. I'm sure she was itching to get to her room so she could call Pat, but curiosity got the best of her, and she stood rooted in front of me like a kid at the zoo waiting to see what the monkeys will do next.

"How was dinner?" I asked, turning the tables on her.

"Fine." She simply smiled and changed the subject back to me. "I made some popcorn if you'd like to eat some with me."

"Sure," I said, pulling the chocolate-covered cherries from my pocket. "Then we can eat these."

Ava's eyes widened, and the contagious smile spreading across her face filled me with happiness. "Cody?" she mouthed. I nodded and led the way into the den, where we sat in front of the large bay window and shared our food.

"Now that Parker's daughter knows he's her biological father, she wants to meet him," Ava said after we'd been munching on snack food for a while. She kept her eyes on the scene outside. From the den, we could see the backyard and a wooded area to the right.

Parker had a daughter he'd never met. She lived in Nevada, and until this past summer, she thought her mother's husband was her real father. Twenty years ago, Parker and his high school sweetheart had planned to marry, but her parents had another idea when she became pregnant. They moved away and married her off to what they considered a more respectable man, who raised Parker's child as his own. Unknown to the daughter, Parker paid for her college. Last summer, the secret came out.

"What does he think about it?" I asked.

"He's excited." She smiled. "Parker would like for me to help them out."

Ava would be the perfect buffer for the pair. Silence fell over the room as we finished the popcorn. It was odd that my sister seemed so hungry for someone who'd just been out to eat, but it was a conversation for another day.

"I've been thinking," Ava said, breaking the silence.

"Oh, no." I feigned a look of horror.

"You know," Ava suggested with a smirk. "We could be knocking up the wrong tree."

"I think you mean barking," I corrected her.

My younger sister had a problem keeping idioms and clichés straight. Malapropism ran in our family. The clinical definition was the mistaken use of an incorrect word in place of a word with a similar sound. She looked at me and rolled her eyes. "Same thing. Anyway, why are you so centered on people in the building?"

My confusion must have been evident because she added, "Your only suspects work in or own the complex where the accountant was killed."

"I'm not," I assured her. "It's just a place to start."

"I see." She nodded, but doubt oozed from her thinned lips.

"What about the ice cream man?" I asked, redeeming myself.

"Ok, then why are you focused only on renters?" The flabbergasted look on her face made me chuckle. She lowered her brow. "I'm sure he had other people in his life."

"True," I said. "In fact, I had a talk with Brynn Rinehart today."

"Oh." Ava arched one brow and leaned closer to me. "What did you find out?"

"Well, she wasn't very close with her uncle." I told her what I'd discovered during my visit beside the pond. "And she was shopping in Placerville at the time of his death."

"By herself?" Ava smirked.

"Yes, she says that's how she prefers to shop." I picked up the box of chocolates and lifted the lid. "I discovered the accountant had a house cleaner and cook, and they didn't come into work until the afternoon."

"That's interesting." Ava took a chocolate-covered cherry from the box.

"Yes." I took one as well and put away the rest for later. "I plan to pay them a visit soon."

"So, the only other renter you haven't spoken with is Chloe." Ava rubbed her chin.

"Now who's zeroed in on renters?" I teased.

Ava shook her head and dismissed my comment with an upward glance. "The last time I spoke with her was at our monthly dinner night."

My sister once ran a salon out of the basement. She'd closed the shop a few years ago, but she and her old employees still got together once a month for dinner.

"How did she seem to you?" I asked, out of curiosity. Although we weren't close friends, I knew Chloe and couldn't imagine her killing anyone.

"Not her normal perky self, to be honest," Ava said, and then her eyes grew wide. "She asked me if the basement was for rent because she couldn't stand her landlord."

"Did she say why?" The accountant didn't appear to have gotten along with anyone.

"No, but I'll see what I can find out." Ava yawned and rose from her favorite chair. "I'm ready to head upstairs and go to bed."

"Good night," I mumbled, letting my eyes droop. A smile tugged on my lips as my thoughts turned to chocolate-covered cherries, Cody, and the memory of his intoxicating kiss.

CHAPTER SIX

"Cut to the chase."

———

The next morning, I woke feeling refreshed and ready to start the day. Since I'd become director of the Calico Rock Mine and Ghost Town, the once dying theme park had experienced a successful turnaround, which allowed me to cut back on my hours. When they'd first hired me, I'd worked seven days a week, temporarily, because those hours were simply too much for anyone. Last month I'd started working half days on Saturdays, staying around until after the stunt shows were over. Before this trouble with the missing money came along, my plan had been to suggest I take Sundays off as well, but now I wasn't sure if I'd even have a job.

When I walked into the kitchen Saturday morning, Ava stood silently staring at the toaster with a look of anticipation. To my surprise, she had on one of her Wild West schoolmarm costumes, and I had to check the calendar to make sure I hadn't mixed up my days. As The Park's schoolmarm, Ava rarely went into work on the weekend. Instead, she tutored students online but could easily rearrange her schedule when something unexpected came up.

"Guess what?" Ava's blueberry waffles popped up from the toaster, and she placed them on her favorite ceramic plate with the flower print.

"What?" I asked, although I suspected whatever it was had something to do with the way she'd dressed this morning.

"I'm getting my hair done this afternoon." She slathered a good heaping of soft butter across the top of each waffle, then looked up, and gave me a sly smile. "And you're going along for the ride."

This was news to me, but since Ava's hairdresser also happened to be one of our suspects, I gave her a thumbs-up. Having her hair done by Chloe was the perfect guise for an interview.

"I'm surprised you didn't mention this sooner," I said while I pulled a box of whole grain wheat flakes down from the cupboard and grabbed a bowl from the counter.

"I just got off the phone with Chloe." Ava set her plate on the table and pulled out her chair.

There were people who considered the chrome-colored seats with metal legs and cushioned back retro, but unless you had a vintage theme going on, the kitchen furniture screamed outdated. My sisters and I really needed to go furniture shopping. Until recently, none of us had had the heart to talk about the elephant in the room. Mom and Dad passed away years ago, and I'm sure they wouldn't mind if we fixed the place up by bringing the decor into the twenty-first century.

I grabbed the milk carton out of the fridge and carried my stuff across the room to join Ava at the table. She squeezed copious amounts of syrup over her waffles, and I suddenly questioned my decision to go with something less sugary. Her face beamed with anticipation as she forked a section of the hot waffle with butter and syrup oozing off the sides and held it in the air as she explained, "Chloe has an opening this afternoon at two, and I knew you'd be off work by then."

Perfect. I caught on quickly to Ava's plan. While my sister got her hair cut, we could have a long talk with one of the accountant's old girlfriends, who seemed to hold a grudge against him. Since I lived with one of the best hair stylists in the county, I didn't need a haircut. Ava had loved being a beautician, but she'd sold her hair salon a few years ago because she said the constant exposure to chemicals was getting to her. Now she was finally using the elementary education degree she'd earned in college by teaching children English online. So long as Ava was working with people, she was happy.

"So, do you want to go into work with me?" I added a generous amount of milk to my bowl and used a spoon to submerge each flake. I liked my cereal on the soggy side. "Or should I plan on swinging by to pick you up?"

"I'll go in with you." Finished with her breakfast, Ava stood and spun around, holding the edges of her prairie costume out, so the skirt bellowed. "I can clean up the schoolhouse this morning, and then we can have an early lunch at the Calico Rock Café."

We both clocked out at noon, ate lunch, ran home to change our clothes, and then jumped into the Jeep. On the way to the salon,

Ava pulled down the passenger side visor, looked at herself in the mirror, and gasped. "Wow, I see gray hairs. I don't know if I should have Chloe do a dye or just add highlights."

"Your hair's not turning gray." I snorted while trying to hold back a laugh. At thirty-six, she looked young for her age and could have passed for a college student.

"Chloe will know what to do," Ava said with a sigh as she closed the visor. "She's great at envisioning the finished results."

"Yes," I agreed. Chloe was about as good as Ava. I loved what she'd done with Pat's hair the last time she'd cut it. Although Ava did my hair, she refused to work on Pat's curly locks, claiming they were too unruly. I think she'd grown weary of our perfectionist sister telling her what to do while she worked. Chloe, on the other hand, nodded at Pat's suggestions and then did her own thing. The short bob she'd given her had softened our older sister's features and had given her a more youthful look. Chloe was quite a bit older than us, but we knew her family from church and had spent a lot of time with them when we were growing up. Her ex-husband had been one of the coaches at the high school. I still remembered their wedding from when I was in junior high school. "I never heard the story of why Chloe and Drew broke up."

Ava rolled her eyes and looked at me. "She had no choice but to divorce him after he left her for another woman."

"Not one of the cheerleaders, I hope." Nothing rankled me faster than hearing news of leaders betraying the trust of the public by misusing their influence.

"No, but she was one of the schoolteachers." Ava's voice was somber yet filled with disapproval. "I don't think you ever knew her. They eventually moved to Indiana and got married. Good riddance to them if you ask me."

Poor Chloe. That had to have left a bitter taste in her mouth. When we arrived at the Rinehart Complex, there were only two other vehicles in the parking lot, Sam's old beat-up truck, and a blue two-door Ford Escort. "That's Chloe's little car." Ava pointed out the window.

From all appearances, Sam wasn't getting any customers, and my heart broke for him. Dad always claimed Sam was the best barber he'd ever had, so it seemed hard to believe the competition could have been good enough to take so many of Sam's customers. He was a town legend in my mind. The man needed someone to help drum up business for his barbershop. Jack kept his hair short. I had no idea where he went to have his cut. I made a mental note to talk with Pat. Maybe she could help get him new customers with the guys at the sheriff's department. Poor Sam, he'd looked depressed the last time I'd seen him, especially before he had realized I'd entered the shop.

When I walked into the building with my sister, I felt an odd sensation. A shudder passed through me as the staircase leading to the second floor drew my attention. I shook away the bad memories and followed Ava past Sam's barber shop and to the Clip N Dye hair salon.

Chloe was in her mid-fifties, divorced, and had no children. Her sister Carrie lived in town and was married to a truck driver named Jimmy Silverman. That's all I knew about Chloe's personal life, other than she'd once worked for my sister as a beautician.

"Come on in, girls." The laugh lines around Chloe's eyes accented the broad smile on her face. "Make yourselves comfortable. Feel free to sit on one of the salon styling chairs."

There wasn't a waiting area with seating, so we sat on the styling chairs.

"As you can see, I really need a bigger place." Chloe pulled a long ivory comb from the front pocket of the pink polka dot smock she wore over her blue jeans and white blouse and pointed in the general direction of the workstations. "I have two other units in storage, but as you can see, there isn't enough room here for all of them."

Chloe wrapped a black plastic salon cape around Ava's neck and attached the Velcro strips in the back. She lifted a section of my sister's dark hair and said, "What are we wanting to do today?"

While Chloe and Ava discussed what to do with her hair, I looked around the room. The decor was basic, nothing splashy or out there. Dark paneling and hardwood flooring seemed to be the theme. The stations lined up on the left side of the room with tall, oval mirrors and black leather rotating chairs that could be raised or lowered as needed. A continuous counter stretching across the wall held supplies for each setting. Two sinks in the back for washings had a supply closet in-between them. There was a tall stool with a white cushion next to a desk by the front door. Since there was a cash box instead of a register, I assumed she preferred credit cards for payment. The layout was basic, without any sort of personality, but as Chloe had said, the space she had to work with was limited.

A few years ago, when my sister closed her business, Chloe had purchased all five of the stations Ava put up for sale. The three in the salon were a tight fit, but not so crowded you couldn't work. If she had a large clientele, it made sense she wanted more space.

"What made you decide to set up your salon here?" I asked as she led Ava to one of the sinks in the back of the room.

"Well, when Melvin and I were dating," she explained after motioning for Ava to lean back while she ran the water over her hand to test the temperature, "he convinced me to take this smaller office downstairs because he was going to remodel upstairs. The plan was for us to eventually be across from each other. Then wouldn't you know it, right after I signed a two-year lease, he dumped me and started seeing another woman. Plus, he dragged his feet about getting the bigger office finished."

After she rinsed off the shampoo, Chloe squeezed excess water from Ava's hair, wrapped a towel around my sister's head, and then had her move away from the sinks and back to the workstation. "I hate to admit it, but I think that man went out with me, so I'd fill a vacancy in his dumb old building."

"It's hard to believe someone killed him." Ava turned the conversation to the real reason for this visit.

"Yes, it is." Chloe didn't sound overly upset by the man's death. If I hadn't known better, I'd have thought she hardly knew him.

When she'd finished combing out the tangles in Ava's hair, she picked up a pair of scissors and gave me a sideways glance. "It must have been horrible for you to find him like that."

"Yes, it was." I assured her. Since finding the accountant's body, I'd had a hard time falling asleep at night. "I noticed you didn't open the salon that morning."

"No, we're usually closed on Sundays and Mondays, but my helper, Jan, called in sick on Wednesday. I didn't have any appointments scheduled,, so I took the day off."

"I guess Melvin's niece will be your new landlord." Like a volleyball pro, Ava kept the ball in our court.

"Brynn's a doll." Chloe stepped back to admire her work. "I think she will follow through with her promises and make right some of her uncle's messes."

"That will make people happy," I said. "It seems like Mr. Rinehart stepped on quite a few toes."

And he'd made a lot of promises he never intended to keep. Sam and Chloe's stories were similar in the fact the accountant built up a dream too good to pass up, and then once they signed a lease, he dumped them.

"You're not telling me anything I don't already know," Chloe began, but before she had time to say more, the sound of sirens and alarms going off filled the room. I started to rise when Chloe motioned for me to stay seated and pulled her cell phone from her pocket.

"Hello?" the noise silenced as soon as she answered her phone. Chloe paused and listened for a moment, then said, "I can't get away anytime soon, but I may be able to have some friends of mine drop it off."

Chloe walked across the room as she spoke and pulled a blue binder from a shelf inside the tall desk by the front door. She glanced in my direction and gave me a thumbs-up. I had no idea who she was speaking with or what she was trying to convey to me, so I smiled.

"Sure, I'll let you know." Chloe then hung up and put her phone away before she returned to where Ava sat. Smiling, she picked up a hair dryer and said, "Speak of the devil."

I made eye contact with my sister in the mirror. Her eyes were as wide as mine. Was Chloe suggesting she'd gotten a call from Melvin Rinehart?

"That was the new landlord," Chloe said as she set the binder aside and then returned to blasting my sister's hair with hot air. She had to raise her voice until she finally turned off the blow dryer. "Brynn needs to see a copy of the renter's manual, and apparently, I'm the only one who held on to theirs. She would come by and pick the booklet up herself, but she's in the middle of something and will head in the opposite direction when she leaves. I have three more appointments this afternoon."

"We'd be happy to run it by for you." I didn't even try to hide my eagerness.

"I had a feeling you might feel that way," Chloe said with an impish grin. She spun the chair Ava sat in and gave my sister a hand mirror so she could see the back.

"I think your hair looks very pretty," I said truthfully. "How do you like it?"

"I love it." Ava swung her head from side to side while staring at her reflection.

"Like I said, Brynn's a doll," Chloe explained, changing the subject. "There's only one thing I'm concerned about."

"What is it?" This time I kept my voice steady so as not to sound too curious.

"She's young and inexperienced." Chloe removed the cape covering Ava and picked up a broom leaning beside the station. "I hope she's not taking on too much."

After Ava paid for the haircut, we thanked Chloe and left the building. The only cars in the parking lot were my Jeep and Chloe's Escort. Sam must have gone home early.

"Oh, wow." Ava's jaw hung open, and her eyes grew wide with awe when we pulled into the driveway.

The accountant's house, which now belonged to his niece, looked like a miniature mansion. A detached three-car garage stood at the top of the drive. Between the garage and house, a covered walkway led to what appeared to be a mudroom or laundry room leading into the house. At the front, a large covered porch with three square Greek pergola-style columns supported the overhanging roof.

I kept an eye out for four-legged creatures since Brynn mentioned the neighbors complaining about dogs barking. There weren't any signs of canines in the yard. As soon as we hit the porch, the sound of dogs going nuts came from inside the house.

"Come on in." Brynn opened the door soon after we knocked. She must have been watching for us. Our host wore a maroon floral sundress with a V-neck and short sleeves and looked ready to go out. At her feet, two Pomeranians darted toward us barking, but retreated before getting close enough to touch.

Ava and I stepped into the house and entered a spacious foyer. Immediately to the right was a den filled with natural light coming in through three side-by-side window panels. On two of the walls there were shelves lined with what appeared to be thick legal books and a table with a computer and rollback chair which turned the room into a home office and spacious library.

"Let me get these two boys in their room so we can talk." She scooped the pair up and pushed a door on the right with her hip before setting the dogs down inside the room she called *theirs*.

"You two behave now," she said, wagging her finger before returning to the foyer. "They have a doggie door so they can play out back if they like."

"Good afternoon," I said and handed Brynn the binder from Chloe.

"I appreciate your bringing this by for me." Brynn gave the loose-leaf folder a quick glance and then tucked it into the brown leather oversized tote bag hanging from her shoulder.

"It's no problem. We were just leaving Chloe's place when you called, and it was right on our way home," I assured her and then motioned toward my sister. "I don't believe you've met my sister, Ava."

"No, I haven't." She reached her hand out to Ava. "It's nice to meet you. I'm Brynn."

"It's nice to meet you too," Ava said as they shook hands.

Looking at both of us, she asked, "Is this your first time to see the house?"

"Yes, it is," Ava answered for both of us.

"Let me give you a quick tour," Brynn said after glancing at the silver and gold watch on her wrist. Encrusted diamonds circling the edge sparkled when she moved her arm.

We both nodded like grade schoolgirls who'd been offered a piece of candy. An open floor plan gave the impression of being in a grand hotel. The state-of-the-art-kitchen had a large center island with a long countertop leading to the dining area, making them flow together. A fireplace took center stage in the great room, and a sliding door on the west wall led to a covered deck with a scenic view.

"I wish I had more time to show you two the rest of the house." Brynn raised her head to look at the ceiling. Upstairs there's a media room, billiards area, gaming area, a wet bar, and four bedrooms, each with their own bath. "I can't believe this is my place. Uncle Melvin had expensive taste."

"It is very nice," I agreed, his tastes were too rich for my blood. The house was beautiful, but I preferred cozy comfort to spectacular splendor.

Brynn headed for the foyer. "I should ask you over sometime when we can visit, and I'll show you the upstairs."

Ava and I followed her, but I wasn't ready to go yet. "Is your cook or housekeeper in today?"

The sound of a vacuum cleaner running somewhere overhead seemed to suggest the answer was yes.

"Louise is here. She's the housekeeper. Her sister, Martha, does the cooking, but she's been out of town on vacation." Brynn shifted the strap of her purse until it sat higher on her shoulder, like a woman in a hurry to get going. "Would you like to speak with Louise?"

"Yes." Pushing the boundaries of a welcome guest, I pressed on, "If she wouldn't mind. By the way, what is her last name?"

"Miller." Brynn pulled her keys from her bag and then called toward the stairs. "Louise, can you come down here, please?"

"Is Miller Martha's last name as well?" I asked, sounding like a nosy news reporter.

"Yes, it is." Chloe glanced toward the second floor, but without waiting for anyone to answer, she opened the front door. "Help yourselves to anything you need." She waved and stepped onto the porch. "You can let yourselves out when you're done."

Ava and I stared at each other and then turned our attention to the staircase. No one was in sight. As if reading each other's minds, we quietly migrated to the den. From the window, I watched Brynn pull away in her convertible with the top down. I stepped back when my sister swung out her arm to stop me. Fearing for my life, I half expected to find a rattler at my feet, but instead, on the floor was an expensive looking beige hand knotted wool rug with a pattern that resembled hieroglyphics.

"Careful where you step," she warned. "The carpet looks expensive."

"Okay." I nodded as we both gawked at the impressive collection of books. These weren't only books on accounting. Mr. Rinehart apparently enjoyed fiction. He had full sets of collections by several well-known authors.

"Some of these are classics." Ava let out a low whistle and ran her hand along a row of books on a shelf near the desk. "I'd love to spend a few hours in here reading a couple of these books."

As much as I loved to read, at the moment, I was more interested in the computer by the window. Whoever had used the workstation last had left the machine running. The plush office chair with wheels squeaked when I sat down.

"What are you doing?" Ava hissed from behind me.

"She said to help ourselves," I reminded my sister.

"Lily, you know you shouldn't pry into other people's personal business." Her voice trailed off as she watched me tapping on the keyboard. From the document's folder, I found one labeled bad client letters.

"Do you have a flash drive with you?" I asked over my shoulder.

"No," Ava snorted. "Why would I?"

"Wait, hand me my purse." I'd used one the other day when the twins wanted me to see pictures from a recent field trip to Placerville. "I have one."

The sound of a woman humming came from somewhere upstairs and grew louder as she moved in our direction. I dug in my purse, better known as the bottomless pit. The large shoulder bag could use a good cleaning, but I kept putting it off since the receptacle would only get messy again. Finally, I felt the small rectangular plastic object I was looking for and pulled it out from the mess.

"Hurry," Ava said. The anxiety in her voice wasn't helping. I dropped the flash drive and had to lean over to search with the tips of my fingers until I located the smooth object pressed up against my left foot. Once I had the drive in the computer, it only took a moment to download the information.

"Can I help you?" A large woman in her mid to late forties stood on the area rug beside the first bookcase. Streaks of gray in her short, dark hair framed her round face.

I swung the chair around as I dropped the drive into my purse and smiled. "Hi, you must be Louise. We've been waiting for you. Brynn said she didn't mind if we asked you a few questions. Of course, it's up to you if you answer them or not."

"Who are you?" she asked as the suspicious expression on her face intensified.

I stood and draped my purse over my arm, holding it close to my body. "I'm Lily Cranston, and this is my sister, Ava," I said, thankful we'd changed out of our period costumes after work, or this woman would have thought we were either nuts or a couple of confused Amish women.

"What did you need to ask me?" Louise crossed her arms over her waist, letting her dust rag hang from her wrist while she kept the other hand fisted.

"We wanted to ask if you had any idea who killed Mr. Rinehart?" I answered honestly, without bothering to beat around the bush.

Her face blanched, and her mouth hung open.

"Lily," Ava let out an exaggerated sigh. "You really need to learn to use some tact when talking to people."

"I'm sorry." Ashamed, I started to apologize more adequately but stopped when the woman raised the palm of her hand.

"No, it's all right. I don't mind." Louise seemed to have regained her composure, although she blinked several times before continuing. "I do not know who killed my boss."

"Did he ever say anything to you about anyone giving him trouble?" I asked.

"Mr. Rinehart didn't talk much to the staff when we were on duty. My sister and I knew what he expected from us, and we did our job," she said with a shrug. "I rarely got a chance to see him since I worked during his office hours. My sister knew him better. She had his meals ready for him before he got home. Many times, she'd cook enough to last days ahead of time. He liked for us to be gone when he returned from work."

"How long had the two of you been working for him?" Ava asked.

"Oh, for several years now." She looked off into space, as if mentally counting. "It's been about eight years."

"Thank you for your time." I took my sister by the arm and pulled her in the direction of the front door. "I'm sure you're busy, so we won't keep you any longer."

"Good day." Shoulders stiff and head held high, she walked us to the door, and I'm fairly sure I heard the bolt lock *click* once we'd stepped out onto the porch.

"What's the sudden rush all about?" Ava asked on our way down the front steps.

"She had nothing for us," I said, although what I really had in mind was to get home and look at the file. Biting down on my bottom lip, I wrinkled my nose and tapped the side of my purse. "But we might find a clue in here."

CHAPTER SEVEN
"Every cloud has a silver lining."

———

Bright and early Monday morning, Gretchen handed me a pile of envelopes the minute I walked in the door. Opening the morning mail was a job she relished, especially when it came time to dispersing the letters to the right person. Around the office, we teased her saying she'd missed her calling as a mail carrier. As the manager, I received a larger number of missives than the other department heads, not because I was more popular but because I got those addressed to me as well as those no one knew what to do with.

I flipped through them and let out a yawn before stuffing the stack in my bag.

"Looks like you stayed up too late last night," Gretchen teased while batting her eyes. "Did you have a date with that handsome C.S.I. officer friend of yours?"

"No, I just couldn't fall asleep," I told her, although after Ava and I both had spent most of the night looking for clues, to no avail, I was exhausted. Mr. Rinehart must have kept his business dealings on his computer at his office. All we learned from our snooping was he was a well-read man who loved reading the classics and taking exotic island vacations.

"Mmhmm." She didn't look convinced.

"You look spiffy this morning," I said, once I realized she had on one of her more colorful outfits. The dark blue scarf and blouse complemented her eyes.

"Robert's coming by to take me out to lunch again," she said with a smile. Since she looked happy, I assumed they hadn't called him back to work. I was about to ask where they planned to go when the front door flew open, and Steve stomped into the lobby. The dark expression on his face could only mean one thing—he had bad news.

"Good morning, ladies," he greeted us both and then turned to me. "I need to see you in private."

"Of course," I said as I led him toward my office. Steve followed me into the room, and instead of taking a seat, he came to stand beside me next to my chair.

"I need you to explain these to me," he said as he waved what looked like several bank statements in front of my face.

"What is it?" I reached out for them, but instead of handing me the sheets of paper, he continued to hold them out of my reach. "This is a copy of a printout Mr. Rinehart wanted to speak with you about."

"Oh?" I was curious to see what incriminating evidence the accountant had discovered since I knew I had done nothing wrong.

"He came across these in his investigation before someone killed him." Steve pointed to the documents, but they were too far away for me to make out the information.

"Can I see the papers?" I raised my hand and waited for him to hand them over to me. After a quick perusal, I found out they showed charges made to the company account going back several months. Each time, the amount taken was small and replaced within a week or two. Apparently, someone had been taking funds out and then putting them back, which made no sense to me.

"They aren't mine," I insisted as I rose from my desk and carried the lists to the copier. "Give me time to look this over, and I'll see what I can do to make sense out of these."

Seeming to be satisfied, Steve gave me a quick nod before putting his hand on the doorknob. Suddenly, he turned and raised his index finger. "Oh, I almost forgot to tell you. We've decided to ask Gretchen to have a look at the reports since she has a degree in accounting. I'll talk to her on my way out."

Filled with frustration after he left, I turned my attention to finding out who was trying to frame me and why. It had to be someone in the company. The thought of any of the people I worked with wanting to either get me fired or put the blame on me hurt. I honestly couldn't think of anyone on staff who I didn't like or got negative vibes from.

After Gretchen called to let me know she was taking her lunch break, I did another search of the bank account activity, and everything looked fine. Until the last large amount taken out in September, the undocumented withdrawals had been small, and the account balanced within a month or two. Since Gretchen used to be a

CPA, I had considered asking her for help myself, but now the decision had been taken out of my hands.

The door at the entrance chimed, and I rose from my chair to greet whoever was there since Gretchen was still on her break.

"It's just me," Pat called out from the lobby.

"Come on back," I raised my voice for her to hear.

Pat had on a blue and white floral dress with short sleeves and large pockets on the sides and a deep V-neck. The dress had always been one of my favorites. She looked stylish, comfortable, and casual. The black sneakers she wore clashed, but hey, when you're comfortable in your own skin, you don't care what anyone else thinks.

"What brings you out this way?" I asked as I watched her drag a chair next to mine.

"I went out to the Farmer's Market to see if they had any fall pumpkins to decorate the yard with for Halloween. It wasn't too far out of my way to swing by here, so I thought I'd drop in and see how you were doing."

"Well, you have good timing." I glanced at the clock on the wall. "My next tour isn't for another hour."

Pat let out a sigh, which was a sign she had something on her mind, so I waited and let her tell me when she was ready. She stared at my computer screen. "What are you working on?"

"You just missed Steve," I said and rolled my eyes instead of answering her question.

"What did he want?" The sarcasm in her voice let me know she was on my side, whatever the reason for the boss's visit. All for one and one for all could have been the Cranston motto.

"He showed me some discrepancies in the account dealing with money going out without a receipt." I still couldn't believe the nightmare of it all. "I convinced him to give me time to research where the money has been going."

"All right then, let's do it." An enterprising individual, Pat was good with numbers and facts, so the perfect person to help me with this task. She rubbed her hands together and then leaned in closer to the computer.

"Okay," I said, happy to have her support. "I'm just trying to figure out where to start."

"How about at the beginning?" Logic was one of her strong points, along with taking charge. She drove me nuts at times, but right now, my big sister was exactly who I needed.

"Great idea," I told her and went to the most recent unauthorized withdrawals I'd found. "In September, we were out of balance by one thousand dollars."

Pat let out a low whistle. "Why don't you explain to me how The Park's account is set up? Banking 101, tell me who gets what."

"Okay," I explained. "Money comes in from guests, sponsors, and donations. I oversee the budget. Based on where it's needed, the funds have to be diverted to pay wages, monthly bills, or go into the emergency account used as needed."

"As needed?" Still looking confused, Pat opened her mouth to say more then abruptly shut it.

As much as I enjoyed seeing her so bewildered, I quickly explained, "Last summer, before the new gold vein was discovered, payments for bills and some of the payroll came out of the emergency fund."

"Ahh." She nodded with a look of understanding. "So, you use it when there's not enough money to pay the bills."

"Yes," I said.

"Who has access to the money besides you?" She posed a good question, but an easy one to answer.

"Well, no one." A spot between my eyes throbbed, but I ignored the pain. There wasn't time to get wimpy. "I pay the bills, make out payroll checks, set up petty cash, and transfer the excess money to savings."

"Do you write the company checks?" she asked.

"No," I told her. "We use the computer to issue checks to the employees and major bills."

Pat nodded to let me know she understood and then asked, "Do they all have your signature on them?"

"No." Her interrogation revealed a weakness in our system. "We use a rubber stamp."

"You have the only stamp?" Her rapid questioning reminded me of her husband. The thought of their greeting one another at the end of a workday with similar rapid-fire responses tickled my sense of humor, but I held back any sign of amusement. I'd wait to share my thoughts with Ava at home.

Reminding myself I didn't want to go to prison, I grew serious. "I have one, and Gretchen has one in case I'm out sick or away from the office during payday."

"Why Gretchen?" Pat tilted her head to the side the way she did when she found something out of place or oddly interesting.

"It's her job to pay small suppliers and deliveries from the petty cash account." I shrugged. "So, it's only natural she'd be the one to fill in for me when I need a backup."

"So." Her brows creased with confusion. "Why isn't Gretchen being looked at as well?"

"Petty cash is a small account," I said. "The most we ever put in there is three to four hundred dollars. Anything larger would have to come to me. The one thousand dollars unaccounted for was taken out on September 7th."

"All right," Pat said and then paused, as if to give the situation a great deal of thought. "Maybe if we think back to what was going on in September, we can come up with something that makes sense."

"Let me think," I said. She had a good idea, and I appreciated her help. I scratched an itch on the back of my head and then pulled up The Park's yearly event calendar. "September was when we had the Worker's Appreciation Day picnic out by the river."

One of the few days out of the year when The Park closed to guests, we threw a party for our employees and their families. The stuntmen performed, and there were horse rides for the kids and other Wild West theme-based entertainment.

"That's right." Pat chuckled under her breath. "I remember."

"What's so funny?" I asked since there wasn't anything humorous about the situation.

"Don't you remember how the youngest of the Bartley girls knocked over one of the punch bowls and soaked your new white boots?"

"Yes." I rolled my eyes and gave her a tight-lipped smile. Cory Bartley played the part of the town druggist. He had three sweet girls, one of which was a bit clumsy at times. "But let's get back to this."

"Okay." Thankfully, she harnessed her amusement and returned to the problem at hand. "Maybe someone forgot to turn in a receipt for the cake or something?"

"No, money for the party doesn't come from this account." We weren't getting anywhere after all. Maybe we were wasting our time and instead should search for countries without an extradition treaty. "It's totally donated by the planning committee. Oh, that reminds me. We also had the community drive for a new highway sign going on at that time."

I grew quiet as I pondered if this had any bearing on the case. Pat gave me her steely eyed stare and waited. "Well?" Pat prodded me to talk after growing impatient.

"It's a dead-end." I sighed. "The donations went right into the safe under Gretchen's desk."

"Why is there a safe under Gretchen's desk?" she asked.

The baffled expression on her face made me grin. "It's where we keep the petty cash, and since she's the one who handles that, the safe is where she can get to it easily when she needs to."

Pat grew quiet, and I looked further back on the report. "Next there was a surplus of ninety-two dollars in August."

"What?" Pat's voice jolted, and her face broke out into a wide grin. "That would play in your favor, wouldn't it?"

"Yes, but it still doesn't explain the missing money." If only the issue were that simple to fix. "July was fifty-eight dollars short, but June balanced to the penny."

Pat shook her head and said, "It sounds like someone is using the account as their personal piggy bank."

"Yes. You're right," I agreed. "Look at this. In May and April, there were two cash withdrawals, each one close to one hundred dollars."

"Wait a minute." Pat's eyes grew wide, and her voice pitched with excitement again. "They didn't hire you until the beginning of May."

"Right, so?" I trailed off at the end of the sentence, waiting for her to fill in the blank.

"That means whoever's been stealing money was siphoning funds before you even worked here." Her eyes sparkled with unshed, happy tears.

After a stunned moment of silence, I blinked the moisture from my eyes and felt a sense of relief seep from my head to my toes.

"You're right," I said as I gave her a quick hug and then turned to my keyboard and started typing.

"What are you doing now?" Pat asked.

"Sending Steve and the rest of the owners a group email," I said without hesitation because I wasn't going to waste any time setting the committee straight. I filled them in on our findings and stopped short of demanding an apology.

Pat watched patiently, waiting until I hit the send button before asking, "So, how are things going with Cody?"

"There's so much going on right now, and we've both been too busy to do much more than talk." When it came to personal matters, I held my cards close to my chest.

"Hmm." She didn't sound convinced. "What about Friday night?"

Ava. I knew she'd call Pat the first chance she got.

"Oh, he stopped by for a few minutes," I said nonchalantly and then switched the topic, hoping she'd take the bait. "Did Ava tell you about her date with Parker?"

A Cheshire grin spread across Pat's face. As always, she was ahead of the game.

The outer door chimed, letting me know someone had entered the building. Most likely, Gretchen was back from lunch, but still I needed to make sure it wasn't one of our guests needing assistance.

"I better check on that," I said to my sister and stood.

"Okay, I need to get going too." Pat walked out into the hall with me. "I guess I'll see you later."

Gretchen and Robert stood near the front door, whispering to one another. He had his face pointed the other way, but Gretchen wore a sad smile. I hoped for her sake he hadn't been called back to work. Robert slipped outside without seeing us approach. Gretchen spun around and gasped at the sight of us.

"Oh, hi." She looked flustered. "I hope I'm not keeping you two from something."

"No," I said. "Pat's leaving, and I have a tour starting soon."

Gretchen seemed oddly quiet, so I asked, "How was lunch?"

"Fine." She gave me what looked like a forced smile. "We ate at the new Mexican place in town."

"I've been meaning to try it." I kept a watchful eye on her expression, and something seemed off. "Was it any good?"

"Yes." She went to her chair, keeping her face turned away from me. "You should give it a try. I think you'll like it. The enchiladas are especially good."

"I will." I joined Pat at the door and waved to Gretchen. "See you later."

If my sister noticed the change in Gretchen's demeanor, she didn't mention it when we left the building. My assistant and her brother may have had an argument or something along those lines. Like they say, when you're with your siblings, you're pulled back into childhood. My sisters and I had had our moments and still did occasionally.

Pat and I strolled along the boardwalk where guests were enjoying a visit to the Old West. As soon as we were alone, Pat tugged my arm and asked, "Who was that young man?"

"Robert, Gretchen's brother," I told her. "He's in town for a while."

"Oh, that's right," Pat said. "I forgot she had a brother. What's he like?"

"He seems nice enough." I shrugged, although I'd really only seen him in passing so far. "But not very talkative."

"It could be he's just shy." Pat sounded like Ava, who always stood up for the underdog.

"You're right." I agreed with her because on the first day we'd met, he'd seemed nervous when his sister had introduced us. When we came to the main entrance, I gave Pat a hug and said, "See you later."

Pat headed for the parking lot, and I strolled down Main Street with a spring in my steps. Feeling relieved and vindicated, I looked forward to giving this next tour since it appeared my job was no longer in jeopardy. It was always interesting to meet the group for the first time because you never knew what you were going to get. Would they be locals, out of towners, or even tourists from another country? I was always up for the challenge.

CHAPTER EIGHT

"To make a long story short."

———

"Did anyone ever get hung around here?" asked a nine-year-old boy with freckles and auburn hair. The nametag on his dark blue shirt identified him as Tommy.

The question came up almost every time I gave a tour, especially when they consisted of a group of fourth graders. The Grady Elementary School sent classes out to tour the mine every month. Last month, I'd entertained a group of first graders who were more interested in The Park's Old Time Candy Shop than anything else. Cute as they were, I preferred working with the older students. Fourth and fifth graders came up with some of the most interesting questions.

"Not that we have any record of," I answered after a hesitant pause, while a gust of wind tugged on my bonnet strings. The wind had kicked up after we began our tour. "But there was an outlaw who once broke out of jail."

"How was that possible?" Their teacher, Mary Porter, brushed a section of her dishwater blonde hair out of her eyes and then clasped her hands together and kept them draped in front of her navy blue dress. "Did he dig a tunnel under his cell?"

Mary and I had known each other since grade school, and I had the feeling the petite schoolmarm was trying to trip me up to see if she could get me to break out of character. So far, her responses to my explanations had been off the wall.

"No," I said, and then as if on cue, the wind tossed a tumbleweed against the side of the jailhouse and bounced down the alleyway next to the bank. With a smile on my face, I brought the conversation back on course. "But Elijah Jonas Wilmington, better known as E. J. the crooked gambler, came up with a clever idea."

One blonde-haired girl standing near me let out a gasp, and her blue eyes grew wide. "My brother's name is E.J. and he's always getting into trouble."

"I'm sure it's just a coincidence, Paula." Miss Porter placed a hand on the child's shoulder.

"Why was he in jail?" asked a sweet little brown-haired girl with a pixie face. Her green eyes filled with wonder.

"Cheating at cards, I believe." This was turning out to be one of my more inquisitive tour groups. I preferred they ask questions, so I'd know they were listening to my stories.

"What did he do to escape?" asked the boy standing next to the one who'd originally brought up the subject. His name tag had the name Brent written in bold red letters.

"While serving a ten-day sentence for disturbing the peace, E.J. arranged for a friend of his to come in the back door when the sheriff and deputy were away," I explained. "They always locked the front entrance when they were out of the office but didn't worry about the back. When the coast was clear, his friend unlocked the cell. Everyone in town knew the lawman kept the keys in the top drawer of his desk."

"Did they catch him?" asked the tallest boy in the group, a green-eyed blond who I suspected was a good two years older than the rest of his classmates.

"No, actually he managed to get away," I explained. "But his friend ended up serving the rest of E.J.'s jail time, plus an additional amount of time for breaking him out."

"What was his friend's name?" Brent seemed to have an unlimited supply of questions.

"He was Jerimiah Grady, nephew of the town founder, Mr. Thomas Grady." Waving my hand, I motioned for them to follow me across the street while I continued, "The whole thing started quite a scandal, and when they released him, Jerimiah left town."

"I bet he found E.J., and then they went to Las Vegas," said one of the students standing somewhere behind me.

"You could be right." I kept my polite tourist guide smile plastered on my face while holding back a chuckle. "I'm afraid no one knows for sure. Let's go visit the blacksmith next."

When I had finished giving the twenty-minute tour of the park to the fourth graders, Sheriff Tom White came up to me. He tipped his hat and shook hands with a few of the children before saying, "Ms. Cranston, there's a problem at the saloon. I think you need to check this out."

Confused, I told the children and their teacher goodbye and followed Tom. Why would they need me at the saloon? The bartender and Tom were better able to handle any problems that came up with the building or customers. When I stepped through the swinging bat wing-shaped doors, movement in the back of the room caught my attention where a crowd of employees stood in front of a table.

"Surprise!" a group of people yelled. Most of them were members of the gang I occasionally ate lunch with at the saloon, Sheriff Tom and his real-life wife, Darla, Dr. Green, and Mr. and Mrs. Porter from the bank station. All but Darla were actors who played important roles to help create an authentic atmosphere for The Park. They'd all become good friends of mine over the past few months.

"What is this all about?" I asked.

They made a path to reveal a large cake on the table with the words *Happy 6 Month Anniversary* written across the top. Bottles of soda, red plastic cups filled with ice, and trays of snack food had been spread out on a table. Touched, I was thankful the odds of me making it as manager for another six months had increased.

"Surprised?" Pat asked, and I had to blink back sudden tears.

"So, this is the real reason you came to visit." I wagged my finger in her face and narrowed my eyes playfully.

"I told you she had no idea." Ava joined us and handed me a plate with a generous slice of cake. She placed her hand on my arm and squeezed gently. "Pat shared the good news with me. I don't know about you two, but I am ready to celebrate."

"Let's not make too big a deal out of it," I said with caution. "Until we find out who is responsible."

"Hey, Lily." Lauren joined us with her camera raised, ready to take a picture. Our resident photographer, Lauren Dillard took pictures for The Park, the local newspaper, and individuals. My best friend since grade school, I was happy to see her in high spirits now that her mother had beaten cancer. "All three of you say, 'cheese.'"

My sisters and I squeezed close together and posed for the picture, and then Lauren let us preview the photo. We'd lined up in order of our ages with me in the middle. The picture wasn't too bad, considering we all had our eyes opened and were smiling.

Pat's face lit. "I'd like to have a copy when you get that printed."

"Oh, me too, please," said Ava with admiration. "You are so good with pictures."

"Thanks." Lauren looked pleased by their response. "I'll make sure all of you get a copy."

Since I didn't have a lot of time to spare, I mingled around thanking everyone for their support and the surprise party while I ate. As soon as I'd finished my cake, I had to return to the office.

After work, Ava climbed into the Jeep and buckled her seat belt before leaning against the headrest. "So, you're no longer under suspicion of taking money."

"It looks that way." Still savoring the discovery clearing me, I smiled.

"What did Steve have to say about it?" Ava asked.

"He called just before I signed out." Our conversation had been short. He'd sounded humbled but also relieved. As an old friend of the family, the situation had put him in a hard spot, and he'd had no choice but to follow the trail, which mistakenly had led to me. "We still need to find out where the money went and who has had their hand in the till."

Ava took out her phone and started scrolling.

"What are you doing?" I asked.

"I'm hungry," she said. "How about we get pizza at the Palace?"

"Sure." Pizza sounded good, and the Pizza Palace was a hometown favorite. "But let's make it to-go. It's been a long day."

"Okay." Ava placed the order online, and ten minutes later, I pulled into the driveway and parked the Jeep.

"I'll run in and get it," Ava said.

She hopped out of the vehicle and crossed the parking lot while I waited in the Jeep. On the corner of Front Street and Main, The Pizza Palace was a popular place for takeout. They really needed to have a drive-thru. While I waited, I sat and watched the traffic stop and go at the light. The road was busy this time of the day with people headed home. A boy on a bicycle with a dog running alongside him waved as he passed. I returned the friendly gesture. We lived in a pleasant little town.

A new influx of vehicles came to the red light and stopped. Among them, I noticed Brynn's red convertible. The top was down, and to my surprise, Ethan was in the passenger seat. Was she giving him a ride or were they a couple now? Around the same age, the possibility of a romance wasn't far-fetched. She was single, and he was divorced. He had his face turned toward her, but I recognized the tattoos on his neck and arms. Like the last time I'd seen him, he wore a black and white bandanna. Brynn threw back her head and seemed to laugh at something he'd said. The light turned green, and they proceeded south on Front Street in the opposite direction of Ethan's ice cream parlor, but toward Brynn's newly inherited house.

Contemplating what this latest development meant, I lost track of time. When Ava opened the door, the savory smell of cheese, tomato sauce, and spices filled the cab. She settled into the Jeep and buckled up.

"Ready?" She glanced at me as if wondering why we weren't moving.

"Yes." I looked over my shoulder and put the Jeep in reverse. The vehicle had a backup guide on the dash, but being old school, I preferred to have my eyes facing the direction where I was going. Once we were back on the road, I cleared my throat and said, "Wait until I tell you what I just saw."

Back at the house, Ava took our food to the table in the living room. I poured us two tall glasses of iced tea and joined her. Ava picked up a slice of veggie lover's pizza, closed her eyes, and smiled as she took a deep breath.

"I wonder if they are dating," she said before taking a big bite. A glob of cheese oozed without separating, so she grabbed a napkin.

"I don't know if they're a couple or not." I'd told her all about my impromptu stake out on the drive home. "Of course, they know each other since he rents a building from her. She looked happy, that's for sure."

Ava washed down her food with a swig from her glass of iced tea. "Maybe they planned the whole thing together."

"The murder?" The thought had crossed my mind, but I had my doubts. Something about the idea didn't feel right. "I don't know. If they'd planned it, you'd think they'd have given each other an alibi. In this case, each of them claims to have been alone at the time of Mr. Rinehart's death."

Cocoa jumped onto the couch and nuzzled against Ava. Hoping for a treat, no doubt. Ava stroked the cat's fur. "What better way to look like they weren't in on the crime together?"

It would have taken me all night to go over the holes in her reasoning, but there wasn't time. Now that I was no longer under suspicion of having taken money from The Park's bank account, I still needed to solve the embezzlement fiasco. Someone had committed a crime, and the committee had yet to call in the police. "I can't help feeling there's a connection between the accountant's death and the missing money."

Of course, I'd never thought they'd actually toss me in jail, but I had been concerned they would let me go, and if so, I'd have to move away from Grady again. Since returning home, I was happier than I had been in a long time, and I never wanted to leave again.

CHAPTER NINE
"A blast from the past."

———

As much as I loved my job, working on payroll was my least favorite thing to do because it was such a time-consuming task. We had paid employees, part-time workers, volunteers, substitutes, and a team of professional stuntmen who joined us two days a week. Since most of them expected to be paid, or sometimes reimbursed, I set aside Tuesdays for making sense out of who gets what for the week. To ease my load, Sheriff Tom took care of giving any tours, while Gretchen took my calls and monitored the website for me.

Like any other Tuesday, I went over the spreadsheet, running down the list of people on the payroll, names I knew well. It saddened me to think that one of them must belong to the person who had apparently been trying to frame me. I paid extra close attention to the names of people in each group. Parker overlooked the maintenance department, which had a crew of five. The office staff consisted of Gretchen, me, and Joyce, who filled in on a part-time basis. There were four groundskeepers as we had an opening for a new head of the department. The general staff referred to the person in charge of individual attractions, such as the saloon, jail house, bank, and so on. The largest group was the reenactors, who worked for general staff members. Then, occasionally, we had workers who filled in for others who could not come in for various reasons. Thank goodness, the miners collected their pay from a special fund overseen by the bank.

When I finished the list, I leaned back in my chair and stared off into space. How and when had anyone taken money from the account since I was the only one with access? There were a few accounts I dispersed funds into, like petty cash, but we made sure every purchase was accounted for and every expenditure had a receipt or my signature. I closed my eyes and pressed my head against the headrest of my chair and let my mind wander over the list until I realized it could be an old employee. Of course! I sat up straight and pulled up a record of all present and past workers.

The list was long, which meant I would have to stay late. I texted Ava to see if she could get a ride home with one of her friends. We lived in a small community, and everyone loved my sister. She shouldn't have any trouble. As I suspected, I heard from her in less than ten minutes.

I got a ride. Will you be home for dinner? Ava asked.

I'm not sure. I texted back. *I'll get a burger from next door.*

The café around the corner stayed open till seven on Tuesdays, so I'd have them deliver something if I got hungry. With Ava's ride home taken care of, I rolled the chair as close to the desk as possible to concentrate on the long list of names. Most of them were people I knew and understood why they no longer worked at The Park. Some had passed on, moved away, or retired. Eventually I came across an ex-employee I'd never heard of—Bob Tomson. Something about the name seemed familiar, but I didn't know anyone by that name.

I opened the individual's folder to read the notes, but the file was sloppily incomplete. There was no sign of a resume, interview transcripts, or their work history. Just a name and The Park's address. The only information on Bob Tomson was the three dates when they'd issued him checks. The first two had been made out for fifty dollars, and the last one written a year later for five hundred. Apparently, he worked for the company on and off during the two years before they had hired me. His pay was sporadic, as if he were a temp who filled in for absent employees.

Gretchen had been an employee of The Park longer than me, so I went to the lobby to see what she knew about this phantom employee, but she wasn't at her desk. I looked at the clock and remembered it was after hours. She'd left for the day. I wanted to write a note for her to call me in the morning, but the front door chimed and in walked Parker, the head of our maintenance department.

"Hello, Lily," he said. One of the company's longest standing employees, he also worked part-time as a sheriff's deputy. A year ahead of me in high school, I'd known who he was, but had never gotten to know him until becoming manager of The Park.

"Hi," I said as I set down the pen and paper. If I didn't get the answer I needed from Parker, I'd check with Gretchen the next time I saw her. "How are you today?"

It crossed my mind to ask him what his intentions were toward my sister but decided this wasn't the time or place to joke about personal matters. Parker was a nice guy, and Ava had come home happy after their dinner date.

"I'm just fine, thank you," Parker said as he held out a slip of paper for me to take. "This is a receipt I need to turn in for the wires I picked up to fix the speakers behind the gazebo."

"Thank you." I dropped the invoice into Gretchen's inbox, and I realized Parker was the perfect person to ask about Mr. Tomson since he'd worked here longer than anyone still employed. "By the way, I wonder if you can help me figure something out."

"Sure." He looked intrigued, with one brow raised and his head tilted slightly. "Sure, what's up?"

Tall and lean with a ruddy complexion, Parker ran a hand through his hair. Dark and wavy, his locks had a frizzled look to them. A nice-looking man with a pleasant personality, I understood why my sister liked him. Or maybe she secretly wanted to get hold of him with a pair of scissors.

"Do you recall there ever being an employee here by the name of Bob Tomson?" I asked.

"No, but the name does sound familiar." One side of his mouth pulled tight as he stared off into space until his eyes lit, and he snapped his fingers. "I know where I've seen the name before. It's on one of the headstones in the ghost town's cemetery."

Then it had to be a strange coincidence, because the only people buried on the property had died over a hundred years ago. Modern day burials weren't allowed in The Park. The phone on Gretchen's desk rang, and Parker waved on his way out the door.

"Hello," I answered without checking the number to see who was calling. "Lily Cranston speaking."

"Hello, Lily Cranston." The sound of Cody's warm voice was a pleasant surprise and filled me with happy vibes. "I hope I'm not interrupting anything."

"No," I assured him. "You're fine."

"I'm near The Park," he said. "And wanted to see if you'd be able to join me for dinner."

"Sure." The thought of turning him down never crossed my mind, and as it stood, his timing was perfect. Besides, who wouldn't look forward to spending time with a man like Cody? "I'll finish up here in about another thirty minutes."

"Perfect." He sounded pleased. "I'll wait in the lobby for you if you're not done when I get there."

Twenty minutes later, I turned off my computer, fixed my makeup, and combed my hair. There wasn't anything I could do about the outfit, but Cody knew when at work I was in character. When I left my office, I found him seated by the front door, focused on the screen on his phone. He didn't appear to hear me when I entered the lobby. His muscular build did a fine job of filling out the white shirt and blue jeans he wore when on the job. Given the chance my thoughts registered on my face, I flipped off the hallway light, sending the back half of the building into darkness. Cody stood to greet me.

"Hello." The dark seemed to add a deep, husky quality to his voice.

"Hi." I took a deep breath to compose myself. "I'll just be a minute. I need to turn off a few things and lock up."

When we were ready to step outside, Cody took my hand and tucked it into the crook of his elbow as we strolled down Main Street. The sun's evening glow had faded into the night, and stars filled the dark, cloudless sky. There weren't a lot of people out on the boardwalk. Alice Stone waved from across the street, where she locked up the candy shop. Tuesdays were slow, and the restaurants would close soon.

"Where would you like to eat?" Cody waved his hand and smiled as if the options were limitless when there were only two choices for a full meal in The Park, The Calico Rock Café or the Watering Hole Saloon.

"Either one is fine with me," I told him.

"Since it looks like we have reason to celebrate," he said with a grin, "let's go to The Watering Hole."

"Celebrate?" I wasn't sure what he meant since he'd have told me sooner if they'd solved the murder. The smell of cedar and pine wafted from the candle shop as we reached the end of the block, where we had to cross the quiet street to reach the saloon.

"I hear you have exonerated yourself." He laid his free hand over mine and gave it a gentle squeeze.

"News travels fast when you're related to Pat Owens," I said with a hint of sarcasm in my voice. Cody looked at me sharply, then relaxed when he realized I was joking. To show my softer side, I gave him a playful smile. At the same time, the heel on my right boot caught on the edge of the boardwalk, pitching my body forward. I was moving in slow motion until I felt Cody's arms come round my waist, preventing me from hitting the ground. I looked up at him. "Thank you. That was close."

"My pleasure," he said, keeping his arm around me the rest of the way.

Piano music spilled out from the building as we climbed the wooden steps and then passed through the swinging batwing doors. I looked around the room while we waited to be seated. There were two men I'd seen around town at one end of the bar talking to one another, and at the other end, our waitress, Trudy, had her elbows resting on the countertop while she chatted with Max, the bartender. Drying off a clean glass, her boss noticed us before she did and nodded in our direction. He must have let her know she had customers because Trudy scurried across the floor and welcomed us to the Watering Hole before leading the way to a table by the front window.

Cody waved to Parker and a few men from the maintenance department sitting in the back of the room. After we'd placed our order, Cody scooted his chair closer to mine instead of sitting across the wide circular table from me, and then he looked at me with those beautiful dark brown eyes of his. "Other than having your name cleared, how did your day go?"

"Just fine," I said. "How was your day?"

"Not bad," he answered quietly. I wanted to dig deeper, see what he had uncovered so far about the murder case. But the subject was a sensitive one that needed to be dealt with prudently.

Cody leaned close enough that I could smell the peppermint on his breath. "Tell me what's new in Lily Cranston's life."

Just then, Trudy brought us our drinks and a bowl of pretzels. I waited until she left to answer. "I ran across something curious while doing payroll this morning."

Cody stared at me in disbelief. "More missing money?"

"No, not really." I explained while watching him take a drink from his glass of soda. "I came across an ex-employee's name which has some odd activity."

He raised an eyebrow and looked at me. "Odd?"

"Yes." I used my straw to stir the ice cubes in my sweet tea. "Sporadic payments and an incomplete file."

"Is that strange?" Cody looked puzzled as he took a pretzel and broke the crispy bite in half before popping the smaller piece into his mouth.

"Yes, it is. And it gets even stranger." I paused long enough to gather my thoughts. "According to Parker, the name matches one on a headstone in the graveyard."

"Now, that does sound odd." Cody nodded in the direction beside me to let me know Trudy was coming with our food. He moved his glass aside to make room for the plates she set in front of us. We'd both ordered the daily special—cheeseburgers and fries.

"Thanks," we said at the same time and then laughed.

"You're both welcome." She grinned. "Let me know if you need anything else."

I waited until we were alone again to continue but, for some reason, still felt the need to lower my voice. "What do you know about the managers who worked at The Park before me?"

I figured Cody would know as well as anyone else since he'd been overseeing and assigning stunt-duty officers from the start of the program. For several years now, he'd taken on the role of safety officer as a volunteer. It was high time we acknowledged The Park's wonderful unsung heroes. The next time I spoke with Steve, I'd bring it up. There had to be some way we could pay back people like Cody.

"It's been awhile," Cody said and paused as he gave it some thought. "Wasn't Wade Womack The Park's first manager?"

"Yes, I was still living here in Grady back then," I said while squeezing ketchup onto the side of my plate.

When The Park came to be established as a money-making business, I'd still been in high school. Born and raised in Grady, Mr. Womack had helped create the committee that still ran the theme park today. A carpenter, he'd also overseen much of the renovating of the old ghost town.

Cody was salting his fries when I asked, "Whatever happened to him?"

"I think he retired and moved to Florida," Cody said before a commotion at the bar drew his attention. His voice trailed off as he kept talking. "It's been so many years ago."

The two men talking at the far end were getting loud, and the taller of the two slapped his hand against the other one's back hard enough to make the man stumble backward. Max marched over to them and said something we weren't able to hear on this side of the room. The two men waved him off and laughed over what appeared to be a private joke.

"He might not even be alive now," I said, once the commotion had calmed down.

"That's right." Cody looked back at me and pointed in the air. "I remember hearing he passed away a while back."

"Who took over after him?" I asked while watching Cody take a bite out of his cheeseburger.

"Jessica Johnson." Cody spoke around a bite of food. There was no ketchup on his plate. Apparently, he ate his fries au natural. My sisters teased me about my obsession with the condiment, saying ketchup was for kids.

"Are you sure?" I picked up my cheeseburger, savoring the smell of melted cheese. "I don't remember her."

"Yes, she took over a few years after you left town. Jessica was the one who convinced the committee to add the stunt shows." Cody watched one man from the bar walk toward the entrance. "For some reason, she didn't last long after that."

"Do you think he's had too much to drink?" I asked. We made it a policy not to let our guests leave the saloon if they were too drunk to drive. Max kept a close eye on his customers and more than once had had to restrain someone from leaving when too intoxicated to think straight.

"No, he looks all right." Cody gave the bartender a brief nod before giving me his full attention.

"Tell me about Jessica Johnson," I said. During the time I'd been working out of state, I'd only returned home to spend Christmas with my family. "Do you think she'd do something like this?"

"I doubt it," Cody said. "She was a *get the job done* type of person but didn't strike me as an embezzler."

"Just what are the characteristics of an embezzler?" I teased.

"You think I'm kidding?" Cody grinned and then turned serious. "There is such a profile."

Intrigued, I pushed my empty plate away and laid my hands and forearms on the table. "Tell me more about the embezzler profile."

"Well, usually an embezzler is a woman in her late forties who doesn't have a criminal record and is living above their means," he explained. "And of course, they have to be in a situation where they have easy access to funds."

"I'm not in my late forties." I had a bad habit of speaking my thoughts aloud sometimes.

Cody placed his hand over mine. "And you're not an embezzler either," he said with an air of confidence.

"Since Jessica didn't last long, there must have been someone else before they hired me." I spun the conversation back to the subject at hand. "Susan Kingsbury, I believe."

"That's right," Cody said and then took a moment to wave at Parker and his friends as they left the bar.

"What ever happened to Susan?" I asked after his friends were gone.

"Let me think." Cody glanced at his watch. It was getting late. We were the only customers left in the bar. "Last I heard, she got married and moved to Montana or somewhere up north."

The piano music stopped, but the employees still on the clock showed no signs of wanting to close yet. I finished off the last of my tea and let out a sigh of satisfaction before saying, "So, that must mean her departure had been personal and had nothing to do with her work at The Park."

Cody shrugged. "I never heard anything one way or the other."

"Any leads on the accountant?" I knew he wouldn't say even if he did, but you can't blame a girl for trying.

"Not anything I can discuss," Cody pointed out with a grin as he shook his head. He wasn't easy to crack. Actually, he'd never shared anything confidential with me before.

"I saw something interesting last night," I said, shamelessly fishing for information.

Cody's gaze held mine while he waited for me to continue. Since we'd been friends for almost three decades, you'd think my heart would have grown immune to the pull of those mesmerizing eyes of his.

I cleared my throat and then said, "Brynn and Ethan were riding around in her convertible the other night."

"Lily," he started, but stopped when I raised my hand and said, "Just so you know, I wasn't investigating. I was just waiting in the parking lot of the Pizza Palace for Ava to get back with our dinner."

Trudy came by with our bill, and Cody handed her his card, waiting until she left to respond to my news. "It sounds like she was giving him a ride. There's nothing wrong with that."

"No, there isn't, but," I said with emphasis on the word *but*, "Brynn had the most to gain from her uncle's death."

Trudy brought back Cody's card and the receipt. He handed her a generous tip.

"Thanks, Cody!" She smiled as she stuffed the money into her apron pocket and headed in the direction of the bar.

When we were alone again, Cody looked at me and shook his head. "Brynn's alibi checked out."

"Really?" I breathed out sharply. "I thought she was out of town on her own."

"She was." Cody stood and pulled my chair back for me. "But time stamps and video captures verify she was where she said she'd been."

This new information ruled out Brynn as the murderer, but it didn't mean she wasn't an accomplice to the crime.

"How are the boys doing?" I changed the subject as we left the saloon. Cody's "boys" were adults, and like any proud father, he loved to brag about them. The temperature had dropped while we'd been eating, and The Park was empty.

"Now, there's something we can talk about." Cody took my hand as we strolled toward the exit.

CHAPTER TEN
"A penny for your thoughts."

————

On Wednesday afternoon, I drove into town to take some promotional packages to the post office. It was one of those beautiful autumn days when the weather was warmer than usual with a gentle breeze that counterbalanced the rise in temperature. There weren't any tours on my schedule at The Park, and even if there had been, Sheriff Tom could handle any impromptu requests that came up, so I took my time cruising along Main Street with my windows down.

My favorite time of year, I brushed away all negative thoughts and let the fresh smells of fall fill my senses. The musky sweet scents of crisp, sharp decaying leaves and other autumn foliage transported me to comforting childhood days when I was out trick-or-treating with my sisters and our friends. Those simpler times had filled me with love and a sense of adventure, like camping out in the backyard roasting marshmallows with the family. With Thanksgiving coming up, followed by Christmas, the end of the year just kept getting better. Or at least it had seemed like it way back when Dad and Mom were in charge, and my biggest concern had been keeping my sisters out of my candy stash.

I parked the Jeep on Main Street and walked up the block to run my errands. There was a line at the post office, but it didn't take me long to finish my task, so I headed over to the ice cream parlor. It did not surprise me to find the shop still closed with a message on the door to let customers know the parlor was under construction. Outside the building, the street was quiet, and no one else was on the sidewalk. I pressed my face against the glass. It was dark, and there didn't appear to be anyone inside.

Still not in any hurry, I took my time walking to where I'd left the Jeep. Behind the wheel, I turned on the engine and made a U-turn. Headed back in the direction of work, I slowed down as I neared the city park. There was a familiar looking older gentleman sitting on a bench under the oak trees, tossing breadcrumbs to the birds. It was Sam. Curious as to why he wasn't at work cutting hair, I pulled into the entrance and found a shade tree to park under, near the path leading to the pond.

My pioneer era boots crushed the leaves and twigs with loud snapping sounds as I walked. Good thing I wasn't trying to sneak up on him. "Hi, Sam," I said when he looked in my direction. "How are you doing?"

"Fine," he said as he brushed his hands against his pant legs, and his face brightened when he seemed to recognize me. "What brings you out this way, Miss Lily?"

"I had some errands to run in town and noticed you sitting here," I told him and then glanced at the bench. "Do you mind if I join you?"

"Of course not." Sam scooted over to make room for me to sit next to him. "It's nice out here in the fall."

"Yes, it is. The temperature can get a bit too hot in the summer," I agreed with him while I had my eye on a couple of mallards swimming on the opposite side of the pond.

"The ducks are lovely," Sam said. He seemed to be keeping an eye on them as well.

"They're fun to watch," I admitted, although I couldn't recall the last time I'd paid any attention to a flock of birds doing their thing.

Sam looked my way for a moment and then asked, "Have you ever wondered why they hold their tails above the water like that?"

I hadn't really thought about it before, but to be polite, I said, "No, why do they?"

"It's so when unexpected trouble comes their way, they can spring right out of the water and take flight," he informed me.

We'd been watching the birds for a while when my attention strayed to the section of Main Street across from us on the other side of the water. In the distance, the building Sam had once used years ago to cut my dad's hair was visible from where we sat. They had turned the space into a modern family hair salon. I didn't think it was a coincidence that Sam sat where he could see the old shop and recall the golden days of his life.

"How long have you been cutting hair from your new location?" I asked.

"Since Rinehart opened the complex," Sam said with a trace of bitterness in his voice. "He was full of promises and swore moving my business to the new building would be one of the best decisions I'd ever made."

"I remember when you had the shop on Main Street." The sweet memories of time spent with my father had stayed with me over the years. It would have been nice to be able to walk into the old barbershop to see and sense it as it had been back in the day.

"Those were some good times," Sam said, closing his eyes for a moment. "I had customers waiting in line when I was on Main Street."

"It was a great hangout, as I remember." I smiled, trying to lift his spirits. "Dad used to talk about Saturday mornings with the boys at Sam's place."

A wistful smile lit his face, only to morph into a frown. "I never should have listened to Melvin Rinehart. He was a liar."

Sam's face had turned bright red. The anger in his voice was both intense and surprising.

"He owned both places." Sam lowered his voice and took a deep breath as if fighting to remain calm. "He was the landlord of my shop on Main Street, but said he wanted me to be one of his first renters at the new place."

"Oh," I said, surprised. This was news to me. I had no idea Mr. Rinehart had owned multiple buildings. There was the new complex, the ice cream parlor, and Family Hair Salon. "I didn't realize he'd rented out so many different pieces of property."

"Yes, he did." Sam didn't look or sound impressed. "As soon as I moved to the new building, he rented the old one to the folks who own Family Hair Cuts."

It sounded as if he believed Mr. Rinehart had tricked him into giving up a prime location for the competitors. If that were the case, he had every right to be upset. Could he have been mad enough to seek revenge?

"The day Mr. Rinehart died, you said Chloe's was closed," I reminded him. "But there had to have been someone around. I had spoken with him on the phone shortly before what would have been the time of his death."

"You talked to him the morning someone killed him?" Sam rose from the bench. He stood in the shadow of an old oak tree, and the look on his face was hard to decipher. Was it fear?

"Yes," I said. "He called me on the phone."

Sam's face paled, and he returned to his spot on the bench. "Did he say anything about anyone knocking on his door?"

"No, he just told me when he wanted to see me," I answered with caution, concerned by the change in his demeanor. "I didn't hear anything that suggested there was a problem. Was someone knocking on his door?"

"I'm not sure." He shook his head, and a faraway look shadowed his eyes. "There was a loud noise, but I'd gotten used to all the banging sounds from the construction crew. I didn't think much of it until later, when I remembered the workers were taking the day off."

"Do you recall what time it was when it happened?" It must have been the killer he'd heard.

"Around half-past eleven, I guess." Sam's hands trembled as he fumbled to pick up the sack of breadcrumbs he'd used to feed the birds, and then he rose from the bench a second time. His gaze landed in the direction of the Family Hair Cuts center on the other side of the pond. The troubled man's gray eyes narrowed for a moment before he turned back to me. "If you want to know more about Melvin, you should talk to Chloe. Now, there's someone who wanted to see him dead."

"She told me they had dated at one time." I wanted to see if he had anything to add to what I already knew.

"Yes, but the two of them fought like a couple of cats and dogs." He smirked. "He told me they broke up because they didn't get along, but to hear her tell it, he dumped her as soon as she signed the lease."

Other than the part of them having a volatile relationship, his story matched Chloe's.

"I've got to get back to the shop," Sam said and turned to walk away. "Have a nice day."

"You too," I said and waved. "Goodbye, Sam."

I remained seated and watched him walk across the grass to his truck in the parking lot. His confession startled me. The first time I'd spoken to him about the murder, he'd insisted he hadn't seen or heard anything. Hearing a sound wouldn't identify the killer, but still, Sam was hiding something. Mr. Rinehart had taken advantage of him and most likely ended his career as a barber. If anyone had reason to loathe the accountant enough to want to see him gone, it was Sam.

"How was your day?" Ava asked as soon as I climbed into the Jeep. I'd had to stay later than expected to finish up a report the planning committee wanted before morning. So she wouldn't worry, I'd texted her that I'd be late.

"Fine." I appreciated how accommodating Ava was about my hours. If I had to stay late, she never complained. "Have you been waiting here long?"

"No, I figured you'd be along soon, so I came out here to read while I waited." She raised the book in her hand for me to see. We both loved mysteries, and I recognized the cover from one of her favorite author's newest books.

"Good," I said and then turned on the engine. After we'd left the parking lot and crossed the bridge, I glanced her way. "Do you recall an employee with the name of Tomson working at The Park a few years ago?"

Ava wiggled her shoulders and tilted her head to show she was thinking.

"His full name was Bob Tomson," I said, hoping to help jar her memory.

"No, I can't say I've ever heard of anyone by that name," she finally answered. "Do you know what station he worked in?"

"No," I said, disappointed but not surprised. If Parker hadn't known an employee with the name, it wasn't likely Ava would have either. "It looks like he may have been a temp."

She looked at me with a curious expression on her face. "Why do you want to know about him?"

"His name is on the employee list, but his file isn't complete, and his pay history seems odd," I explained. "I spoke with Parker, and just like you, he never met the man, but says he's seen the name on a headstone in the cemetery."

"Oh, my, how strange." Ava got on her phone and started scrolling, googling the name as I had earlier. I didn't think she'd find anything. By the time we reached the house, she sighed and turned off her internet in defeat.

"You know we're going to have to visit the cemetery and look for the marker," Ava said, as if she'd read my mind.

"Sounds like a plan." I turned off the engine and climbed out of the vehicle. "How about on our lunch break tomorrow?"

"Sure, we can bring our food and eat at the schoolhouse," Ava suggested as I unlocked the front door. Her workstation was closest to the cemetery and had a picnic table under a shade tree next to the playground.

After dinner, we took our drinks into the den to watch the sunset. All that remained of what used to be an orchard were a few grapevines and an apple tree, giving us a clear view of the rolling hills behind the house. Cocoa curled up on Ava's lap, and I leaned my head back against my favorite chair.

"I spoke with Sam today," I said.

"When?" Ava continued to gaze out the window as she stroked the cat's fur.

I closed my eyes and let my body sink into the soft, cushioned furniture. "I had to run to the post office this morning and saw him sitting in the park feeding the birds."

"How's he doing?" Ava spoke around a yawn.

"He seemed lonely and sad." The memory of the older gentleman tossing breadcrumbs to the birds tugged at my heart. He had to have friends, if not any family members living. He'd been an icon of the community for over forty years.

Ava was quiet for so long, I opened my eyes and glanced at her.

"Oh, that's terrible." Her bottom lip puffed out, and her eyes filled with moisture. "We need to have him over for dinner one night."

It was a good idea, but I still wanted to be cautious. "Yes, after we solve the murder mystery," I said before closing my eyes again. "We'll invite him to eat with us on a night the twins are over. Sam seems to enjoy children."

"You don't really suspect him, do you?" Ava's chair creaked. I opened one eye and discovered she'd turned to look at me.

"No," I said as I shook my head and sat straight. Since the conversation had turned to the case, I took my notebook out of the side table drawer. "I just can't imagine Sam killing anyone."

"Poor man, it can't be easy for him without any family." Ava was right. As far as we knew, Sam didn't have any living relatives. His wife passed away from cancer and his son died years ago in a car accident. I never heard anyone mention Sam having any brothers or sisters. If he did, they didn't live in Grady.

I flipped the pages until I reached the one with Sam's name at the top and then picked up my glass of tea. "He seemed pretty bitter about the accountant tricking him into giving up his original shop space."

"What Mr. Rinehart did to poor Sam sounds like dirty drool," Ava said with an angry expression on her face.

I came close to spitting out my drink. Just when I thought I'd heard all my sister's crazy, mixed-up idioms, she surprises me with a new one.

"Pool," I corrected her. "It's dirty pool, not dirty drool."

"Does it matter?" She wrinkled her nose and rolled her eyes. "They're both terrible."

"The phrase doesn't refer to saliva or even a swimming pool." I shook my head, although she'd made a good point. "But playing on a pool table unfairly."

"Sam's such a nice old man," Ava said, bringing the subject back to the case and shutting down my attempt to enlighten her.

"Until I can rule him out, he must be a suspect." I jotted down a few notes to remind myself of the conversation with Sam at the city park. "He had opportunity and a motive."

"If you ask me," Ava said as she put her recliner back in an upright position and set the cat on the ground, "Brynn still has the strongest motivation with Ethan in second place, while Sam had the best opportunity."

"What about Chloe?" I asked.

"I don't believe she did it." Ava frowned and looked off into space, as if trying to consider the possibility of her friend being guilty. After a moment, she shook her head adamantly. "She was at home sick at the time of the murder."

"Her helper was the one who was sick, so she decided not to open," I corrected. "Chloe was feeling fine."

"It could be any of them." Ava stood and stretched her arms over her head. "I'm going to bed. Good night."

To keep the peace, I didn't mention what Sam had said about Chloe and Melvin fighting during the time when they were dating. Ava was right. Brynn was the only one of our suspects with a solid alibi, but I wasn't convinced she hadn't been working with Ethan. They both benefited from her uncle's death. I took my glass to the kitchen and rinsed it out before climbing the stairs to my room. It had been a long day, and we were no closer to solving the case. I crawled into bed, closed my eyes, and smiled because thankfully I was no longer under suspicion for embezzlement.

CHAPTER ELEVEN
"Confession is good for the soul."

————

"You know, we should come out here more often." Ava raised her hand to shield her eyes from the bright afternoon sunlight. "It's full of history, and there's a lovely view of the river to the east."

She was right. The Calico Rock Cemetery wasn't off limits to tourists, but the half mile uphill walk discouraged most of our guests from making the hike. Maintained by the grounds department, it was a pleasant area once you reached the two acres on top of the rise. In the future, I'd see about adding a wagon ride to the area once I came up with a way to implement the trip without seeming disrespectful.

"It really is a nice cemetery." I wish we'd been able to wear sunglasses, but it was against company policy while we were on the job in costume. Even though they were around back in the day, the committee felt they were too modern a look for The Park.

Because we were walking around in a graveyard from the late 1800s dressed in clothing worn by women during that era, we may have appeared as ghosts to anyone watching. On our lunch break, we were eager to see what we could find out about the mysterious employee.

"What's the name we're looking for again?" Ava asked.

"Bob Tomson." There seemed to be more rows of headstones than I remembered. "I wish I'd asked Parker for better directions."

There had to be over a hundred plots out there, and the original townspeople had not laid them out in any sense of order other than the Grady's family plot. They'd buried the founder of Calico Rock and his relations on the west side of the grounds under a crop of shade trees. Ava and I didn't expect to find the mysterious headstone there, but if all else failed, we'd save it for last.

"Look at this one." Ava pointed to a tall thin monument with an angel on top. "Alice B Moore beloved daughter and aunt died in 1902 at the age of 12."

"How sad." My heart broke for her parents. "She died so young."

"Pretty young to be an aunt, too," Ava added.

"Yes, back then, many people had big families." My sisters and I were close in age, so the concept was hard to grasp. "It wasn't unusual to have an older sibling old enough to be your mom or dad."

"Here's an old one." Ava read the inscription aloud, "'Joshua Jones died in the flood age 46 years old.' I wonder if it was the same flood responsible for wiping out the original location of the town."

"It probably was, but it's hard to say since there isn't a date on the marker." If I didn't keep her focused on our mission, we'd be here all day speculating on what might have been. "Let's split up," I suggested.

The townspeople of Calico Rock first settled closer to the river, but one rainy season flooded the buildings, and they'd moved to higher ground closer to the mine. Today, a bridge connected the ghost town to the main road leading to Grady. The most recent death recorded was in 1935, which was around the time the town shut down. For years, after they thought the last of the gold had been mined, a few families hung on trying to make a go of it, but too many of their friends and neighbors had left, making it impossible to earn a living.

We walked on for a spell, reading headstones. The outing gave me a deeper insight into the original landowners. There were a few surnames belonging to well-known families still around town to this day. The Morgan family owned the grocery store at the end of Main Street and could trace their ancestry to the town's founding fathers. They had a large section of family members dating back over a hundred years.

"Oh, look. It's Casper," Ava called from a few rows away from me. She knelt and stroked the cat's gray, tabby-striped fur and then pulled a kitty treat out of her pocket. "Here you go, little guy. I'm glad we got to see you today."

One of our cast members had discovered the cat a few years ago, and the friendly feline was now considered The Park's mascot by the employees. The gray tabby preferred the outdoors and lived in a wooden box the maintenance department crew made for it and had placed under a giant sycamore tree.

After half an hour of walking up and down the rows of graves, my feet hurt. They had not made these boots for walking. My respect for pioneer era women had risen tenfold after my first week in costume.

"Maybe we should head back." Ava came up beside me. Either her feet hurt too, or she'd grown tired of seeing the scowl on my face.

"Let's make our way to the Grady plot first," I eagerly complied, although I wasn't ready to give up so soon. "We haven't checked over there."

Before we reached the main section of the cemetery, we came to a spot where a few headstones lined up with the wooden fence. Obscure and away from the others, I wondered why they seemed out of place. Ahead of me, Ava read several of the markers until she raised her hand and shouted, "I found it."

Under a tall oak tree, the writing on some of the headstones was barely visible. Ava squinted and read the one in front of her aloud, "Bob Tomson born 1845 died 1872."

Although the maintenance department did their best to keep the gravestones clean of mold and debris, age had left its mark on several of the older ones with cracks and faded inscriptions.

"He was so young," I said and did the math in my head. "Only twenty-seven."

"I wonder how he died." Ava knelt beside the stone and brushed fallen leaves from the area.

"There's no telling." Unfortunately, they didn't keep records back then the way we do today. "We can research the name and see if we find anything."

Ava nodded but still looked doubtful.

"What I want to know is how his name ever got on the employee list," I said, still confused and a bit disappointed we'd failed to solve yet another mystery.

Our mission completed, we hiked down the hill and walked past the schoolhouse since there weren't any guests around. The church and schoolhouse were the two stations nearest the cemetery. Neither one got a lot of action, which is why Ava, the schoolmarm, and Ted, the preacher, were both volunteer reenactors and not required to put in any regular hours. We only asked they be available during the times their stations would have been active in the late 1800s.

My sister and I crossed over the tracks used for the train ride. The Park had outfitted real mining ore carts with padded seats and overhead awnings to give our visitors a comfortable tour of the theme park and the surrounding countryside.

"Why don't you come to the office?" I suggested to Ava. "And we can look up those dates and see if we can find out more about our mystery employee slash 'dead for over a century' guy?"

"Sure, it sounds like a plan." Ava walked faster, forcing me to pick up the pace. "We can pull up one of those genealogy sites."

"Right," I said, lowering my voice since there were a few groups of tourists out on the street, and we needed to remain in character. "We have his name, date of birth, and death. That should get us somewhere."

"And we know where he died, or at least where they buried his body," Ava added.

We were still discussing where to begin our search when we entered the lobby and found Gretchen pacing the floor wringing her hands together.

"What's wrong?" I asked, concerned. My first thought was something must have happened to her brother.

"I have to tell someone." Gretchen rushed toward the door as if to go outside. I wondered where she was off to when all the sudden, instead of opening the door, she locked it. Ava and I gave each other a side-eyed look.

"Gretchen, tell us what's going on," I insisted since I'd never seen her like this before. She did tend to be high strung at times but not to this degree.

"Sit down," she said as she remained standing. "I'll explain everything."

Ava and I both took a seat on the visitor's couch beside the receptionist's desk.

"It all started with a pair of shoes." Gretchen let out a heavy sigh. "They were the perfect shade of turquoise to complete a new outfit I'd been wanting to wear."

I looked over at Ava, and she shrugged. Gretchen wasn't making any sense, but all we could do was to hear her out.

"They were on sale too." She continued to pace, taking smaller steps this time as she remained in front of where we sat. "But the sale ended on a Wednesday, and I wouldn't get paid again until the following Friday. Plus, it was two days before my birthday."

She appeared to be having some sort of mental breakdown, so I reached for the phone in my front pocket in case we needed to call for medical help.

"You can't imagine how bummed I felt." Gretchen paused long enough to give me a pleading look as I realized she was baring her soul and confessing to a crime. "I'd just written a check to pay for a delivery, and that's when I got the idea. The petty cash fund always had more money than we needed to cover expenditures. If I borrowed the small amount I needed and put it back in on Friday, no one would notice. Susan was the manager at the time, and I knew she wouldn't care. She noticed I was upset and asked me what was wrong. I explained, and she said to borrow the money. No one would notice, and it wasn't stealing if I put it right back. It had been easy to pull off, and no one had gotten hurt."

My heart sank, and I let go of my phone to give her my full attention.

"Honestly, I'd only meant to do it that one time, but it didn't seem like a big deal. Susan even used petty cash to buy us lunch occasionally," Gretchen said, but had the decency to blush. "But as you can see, there were a few other times when I needed to borrow money to make ends meet, but I always put it back."

"Until you took out one thousand dollars," I added, too stunned to be angry at her for trying to frame me.

"But I didn't take the larger amount of money." She blinked away tears, her eyes pleaded for me to believe her. "How could I have? When I borrowed funds, it was always under one hundred dollars because I put it back on payday. Anything larger would have been impossible to pay back."

"It only explains why the money wasn't put back," I said and pulled out my phone. "We need to call Steve."

"I know." She wrung her hands and let the tears fall.

"What will they do to her?" Ava's voice weighed heavily with concern. She stood, grabbed the box of tissues from Gretchen's desk, and had her sit down between us.

"I don't know," I said, although she had confessed to a serious offense which could result in her being fired or disciplined. It depended on if they wanted to press charges. If what she said was true, she'd paid back what she took. It didn't explain who the real culprit was because I believed her story.

With a heavy heart, I dialed Steve's personal cell number.

CHAPTER TWELVE
"The quiet before the storm."

———

The office was silent when I arrived on Friday morning. There was no sign of Gretchen and I had yet to hear from Steve or any other member of the committee as to what they planned to do about her confession. After I'd spoken with Steve last night, he'd insisted Gretchen go straight to his office at the bank. That was the last time I'd seen or spoken to her. It had been hard to sleep last night, thinking about what was going to happen to Gretchen and her job at The Park.

Unsure of how to proceed, I turned on the lights, picked up the mail, and forwarded the phone to my office. If anyone were to enter the building, the door chime would let me know. If necessary, Joyce was available to help, but I wanted to wait until I knew more about what the committee decided.

Sitting at the desk in my office, I sorted the mail, utilizing the accordion file folder we used to separate the envelopes for each different station. Most of the letters ended up in my slot. Before I had time to finish, my cell phone rang, and I recognized Steve's number.

"Hello." I answered before the second ring.

"Lily." The committee chairman had the perfect bank president's voice, a leader who expected respect from his employees. "I wanted to update you on our decision about Gretchen."

"Of course." I tried not to sound anxious or too concerned. One thing about Steve and his team, they were professional when dealing with work-related issues.

"The committee has placed Gretchen under review," he said, and I heard a door shut on his end of the line as if he wanted privacy. "We have suspended her until next week, and regardless of whether we reinstate her or decide to terminate, she will no longer handle petty cash or any other type of money concerns. I'm sure you understand they want to keep the whole issue quiet until we can verify her claims about how the money was used."

"You don't believe she is responsible for the larger amount of missing money, do you?" I asked since that would have meant termination and a criminal investigation.

"No, we don't," he said. "Gretchen has proof she was out of town the day of the large withdrawal and nowhere near a computer or any type of electronic device capable of taking money from the account."

"I'm happy to hear that," I said. "Where was she on September 7th?"

"She took Labor Day weekend off to go on a nature retreat," he said with a hint of a chuckle, which was rare for Steve, but I understood the humor. The image of the company fashion queen roughing it in the wilds was comical. "It would have been impossible for her to have taken the money."

I remembered that weekend. It had been hectic without Gretchen in the office, even with Joyce there to help, because I'd had several tours scheduled one after another. When Gretchen had returned from her trip, she had a load of funny stories to share. I was happy to know they were considering giving my assistant and friend another chance.

Even though Steve didn't say so, I realized this new development put me back in the limelight. Gretchen's borrowing a small amount of money to tide herself over until payday a few times did not account for the one thousand dollars from September that was still missing. So much for celebrating. After I got off the phone with him, I called Joyce to have her fill in for a while. As one of the reenactors who strolled along Main Street, she was prepared to fill in wherever needed. Once I explained Gretchen would be taking some personal time off, she didn't ask questions. I appreciated her discretion in the matter.

Not long after Joyce left on her lunch break, the door chimed, announcing a visitor. I put aside my paperwork and left my office to greet whoever was waiting in the lobby. To my surprise, Gretchen's brother, Robert, stood beside the receptionist's desk, looking at one of our brochures. He wore a pair of rough looking jeans with a gray sleeveless T-shirt. He ran his hand through his hair, clenching his jaw as he shifted his weight from one leg to the other.

"Can I help you?" I asked with concern because he looked upset.

Gretchen's brother set the leaflet down and turned his attention to me. "You're Miss Cranston, aren't you?"

"Yes, I am, but everyone calls me Lily," I said.

"Lily, you've got to hear me out." Apparently, he'd come by to plead his sister's case. Gretchen must be terribly upset for her brother to want to fix things for her. "You can't fire my sister. She's never done anything like this before."

"It's not my call, Mr. Thompson." If it had been up to me, I'd give her another chance, but it wasn't my decision to make. "The committee in charge is going over her case and will make their judgment soon."

"It's not fair that they can just take away her job without hearing her out." There was a look of concern in his eyes as he spoke.

Had Gretchen told him she'd been fired? Her standing with The Park was under review, but she hadn't been let go as of yet if at all. Unsure of what she'd told him, I chose to respect her privacy and stay quiet.

"I'm sure they'll take everything into consideration and come up with a fair verdict," I assured him. There wasn't much more to say or do. "Did Gretchen ask you to come by?"

"No, she'd have a fit if she knew." His facial features soured like someone who'd bitten into a lemon, and then he turned serious again. "My sister loves working here."

I wanted to ask how she was doing, but since I didn't want to give him any false hope, I thought it best to say as little as possible. The man, who had rarely spoken the few times I'd seen him before, seemed to have turned into a fountain of words. He must really love his sister.

"Try not to worry," I told him. "Whatever happens, Gretchen will get back on her feet. She's well-liked around here. Everything will work out."

I felt guilty for giving him any hope when I had no idea what the committee would decide. Before he could respond, a group of actors from the livery stable entered the lobby. We had a break room in the back they sometimes used because, for obvious reasons, they preferred it to their own station. Robert slipped out without saying a word.

Since there was nothing to eat at the house, Ava and I ran into town to do our grocery shopping after work. I told her about Gretchen's brother stopping by the office to plead her case.

"Oh." Ava pushed her bottom lip out into a pout. "That's so sweet and sad all at the same time."

"I know," I said with a sigh since the whole thing was so depressing. "I wish I could have given him good news, but it's out of my hands."

"They should make their decision soon." Ava waved out the window as we passed a group of teenagers selling cookies to raise money for the school's marching band.

"What sounds good for dinner to you?" I asked since most likely she would be the one doing the cooking.

"How about chicken and rice?" she suggested. "It's quick and easy to make."

"Sure, it sounds fine to me." I wasn't all that hungry and really didn't care one way or the other. I knew whatever she made would be good.

There were only three other cars in the parking lot at Price Chopper. I pulled into a spot close to the front of the building and turned the engine off.

"Look who's here." Ava unbuckled her seat belt and jumped out of the Jeep as Chloe pulled up beside us in her blue Ford Escort.

"Hey, fancy seeing you here." Ava grinned as she waited for her friend to exit the car.

"Hi." Chloe slid the pink sunglasses she wore up onto her hair like a headband. Her shades matched her skirt and blouse. "I need something to fix for dinner."

"Us too." Ava burst out laughing. "We decided on chicken and rice."

Chloe's eyes widened with interest. "Oh, that sounds yummy."

"Why don't you join us?" Ava offered. "There's no sense in you cooking the same thing when we'll have plenty."

"All right," Chloe gave in without any resistance. She seemed pleased with the invitation, but then who wouldn't? Ava was an excellent cook and a fun host. "I have some chocolate frosted brownies at home. They were a gift from Sally at the bakery. She loved her new haircut. It was sweet of her, but I can't eat them all by myself. I'll run home and get them for us to have for dessert."

"Great." Ava started for the store entrance and then added, "I'll call you when we're headed back to the house."

Chloe waved and returned to her car while Ava and I went inside to shop. I pushed the cart while my sister picked out the ingredients she'd need for dinner, along with a few other things we were out of at home.

"I hope you don't mind that I invited her," Ava said as we strolled down the sugar and spice aisle on our way to the meat counter.

"Of course, I don't mind," I assured her. "Chloe's always been fun to have as a guest."

"And you'll get to spend more time finding out if she knows anything about the murder." Ava gave me a knowing glance before giving the packages of chicken in the meat department her full attention.

After dinner, the three of us took the pan of brownies and tall glasses of milk into the living room, where we could sit on the couch while we talked.

"I love Sally's Bakery." Ava cut the chocolate goodness into squares and handed them out. "The blueberry muffins she makes are to die for."

Since Ava had set the stage, I said, "That reminds me, I haven't heard anyone mention a funeral for Mr. Rinehart."

"There won't be one," Chloe said as she broke her brownie in two and raised half to her mouth. "According to Brynn, her uncle's will stated he wanted to be cremated without any fanfare."

"That seems odd," I said, unable to keep the shock out of my voice.

"Why?" Ava asked and then pointed to her lips to show I had a milk mustache.

I grabbed a napkin and explained my thoughts, "He struck me as someone who'd want to be honored and remembered for his outstanding accomplishments."

"Melvin wasn't shy, that's for sure," Chloe said. "But he was also unpredictable. He dumped me for a younger woman without any warning."

This news surprised me because the man had been about the same age as Chloe.

"Do you know who his new girlfriend was?" I asked.

"His cook, of all people," Chloe answered with an expression of disgust on her face, and I somehow managed not to choke on my brownie.

"Martha?" Ava looked as surprised as I felt. She set down the piece of brownie she'd been taking a bite out of and gave Chloe's arm a gentle pat. "I'm so sorry."

"You know Martha?" Chloe looked hurt, as if Ava had some part in the scandal.

"No, I've never met her, but Lily and I talked with her sister when we dropped off the manual for you."

"Oh, that's right," Chloe said. She appeared to be relieved. "I forgot I'd sent you both over there."

"She's worked for him all these years, and they just recently hooked up?" My choice of words earned me a glare from my much more tactful sibling.

"I'm sorry," I muttered, feeling chastised, and then added, "It just seems so odd."

"It sounds crazy, I know." Chloe looked angrier than upset. "After we broke up, I learned they'd been having an off-again, on-again relationship for years."

"Martha wasn't there the day we went by," Ava explained again. "We met her sister, the housekeeper."

"Louise," Chloe said. "She's a hard worker. I often wondered why Martha had so little work to do while her sister did all the cleaning in that big house. Martha set her own schedule, coming and going as she pleased. Then when I discovered the affair, I understood all too well what was going on."

"I really wanted to meet Martha," I said. "But from what we'd gathered, she was out of town and Brynn said she had been so for weeks."

It had to have been hard for Chloe to work in the same building as the accountant for those last few months before his death.

"I'd already been looking for a new place to run my business when he was killed," Chloe said, as if she'd been reading my mind.

Until this recent development, I hadn't considered Chloe as a strong suspect, but since her husband left her for a younger woman too, maybe she'd taken it out on Melvin.

"When was the last time you saw Mr. Rinehart?" I asked, although as I expected, my question earned me an exasperated glare from Ava.

"I'm not sure. Let me think." Chloe let out a sigh and raised her face toward the ceiling before looking back at me. "I avoided him as much as possible by having Jan take care of anything that required talking to Melvin."

The room grew silent with anticipation as she continued to think. I wondered if it was really all that hard for her to remember or if she was trying to cover something up.

"Oh, I remember now." She snapped her fingers and nodded her head. "The day before he died, I saw him talking with Sam in the foyer."

"Were you able to hear what they were saying?" I asked, hoping for some kind of clue or a lead to solve this case.

"No, they were too far away from where I stood outside the salon," she said. "But Sam didn't look happy."

No doubt. The accountant was a constant reminder to the barber of what he'd lost.

"Brynn and Ethan are dating," Chloe informed us out of the blue. "Now, there are two people who had a lot to gain from Melvin's demise."

I suspected she wanted to change the subject and didn't blame her. Still, I had a new name to consider with the news Martha had been dishing up more than just meals for the accountant. It's amazing what you can discover through social media. Knowing just how far "out of town" she'd been, and apparently still was, could be important to the case. It looked like Melvin Rinehart's murder wasn't going to be solved anytime soon, with new suspects coming out of the woodwork every day.

CHAPTER THIRTEEN
"Leave no stone unturned."

———

If Ethan and Brynn were a couple, and by all appearances they were, the two of them could have conspired together to kill her uncle for the money. It was no secret that Ethan blamed the accountant for his misery and for good reason. Saturday afternoon on my way home from work, I swung by the ice cream parlor to have a talk with the ice cream man. He'd been very forthcoming the last time we'd spoken, so maybe he'd be willing to give me more answers.

There were only a handful of people on Main Street when I parked my car in the public parking lot behind the Grady Family Restaurant. On busy summer weekends, they needed the space to accommodate all the out-of-town tourists and shoppers. Today, there were only a handful of other vehicles.

I hopped out of the Jeep and locked the door before heading east on Main Street. Rustic buildings maintained the integrity of an Old West town. Concrete sidewalks had replaced the old wooden boardwalk, but the original false front buildings sent you back in time. As much as I'd love to do some window shopping, I was on a mission. I walked past the leather shop and the Grady Thrift Store until I reached Ethan's ice cream store. The shop was closed without any notice of when he'd reopen or if he'd just slipped away for a few minutes. The lights were off, and it didn't look like he'd be back anytime soon.

"Hello, Lily." Belinda Riddle stepped out from the fabric and craft store next to the ice cream parlor.

We were approaching our twentieth high school reunion, and my nemesis looked like she'd been frozen in time. The black skinny jeans with a printed pattern and multi-colored patchwork tunic she wore had been all the rage our senior year of high school.

"Hungry for some ice cream, Lily?" The way she said it made me feel like a twelve-year-old sneaking a cookie from the cookie jar.

"Actually, I'm looking for Ethan," I said, ignoring her snide remark. "I need to talk with him about something. Have you seen him?"

"It doesn't look like he opened today." She peered inside the dark building, as if I'd missed something, and then turned to look toward the other end of Main Street. "But I did see him go into the library just a while ago."

The memory of the large muscular man with tattoos wearing a head bandana flashed in my mind. Belinda must have read the shock on my face. She shrugged and giggled like a teenager. "Why do you look so surprised? He's a regular there."

"How do you know?" I asked. Maybe we had it all wrong about Brynn and Ethan, although he didn't seem like Belinda's type, and she had to be a good ten years or more older than him.

Belinda and I headed in the direction of the Grady Public Library, falling into step and walking side by side.

"Like you, it surprised me the first time I saw him go in there." Belinda placed her hand on my arm. "Remember, my office is right across the street from the library. When work gets slow, I tend to people watch. I can't help myself. Main Street attracts all kinds of interesting personalities."

As the receptionist at the Visitor Welcome Center, I imagine she had a lot of time on her hands.

"Ethan goes to the library a few times a week, believe it or not," she informed me. "Sometimes he even has a lady friend with him."

"One of his daughters?" I asked, digging for more details.

Belinda let out a laugh. "No, she's about the same age as him. She's new in town, but I've seen her around."

"Is her name Brynn?" I asked, in case hearing the name would ring a bell.

"I'm not sure." Belinda shrugged and then made a funny face, like she'd just bitten into a lemon. "You're not interested in him like that, are you?"

"No, of course not." I gasped, with my face matching her sour expression. The man was much younger than me and not exactly my type.

We continued in silence for a few yards. Traffic on Main Street picked up while we were walking. A bus load of high schoolers passed by with the students inside singing one of the school's cheer songs, and I couldn't help smiling.

"Brings back memories," I said to her. "Doesn't it?"

"Yes, it does." She sounded sad, and my heart felt for her. "We need to get together and catch up sometime. It's been so long since we've visited."

At first, I thought her friendly banter meant she was up to something since back in school she wouldn't have given me the time of day. The woman seemed to have a tight grasp on the past, and it was time for her to let go and move forward.

"Sure, it sounds nice," I said and meant it. "Let's have lunch one day soon. Give me a call at The Park Monday where I can check my schedule, and we'll set something up."

We parted ways at the Welcome Center where she worked. I waited for a bus to pass before crossing the street and stopped in front of the library. Two stories tall, wide concrete stairs led to the entrance, where a miniature version of a marble lion on a platform welcomed readers. The architect must have had the New York City Public Library in mind when he designed the entrance. I held onto the wrought iron handrail as I mounted the steps.

Inside in the lobby, Mrs. Kessler sat behind the check-out counter looking at something on her computer screen. The elderly woman had been the librarian here for as long as I could remember. The heels of my boots made a loud sound against the polished tile floor, and Mrs. Kessler peered over the rims of her bifocals. I squinted my nose and mouthed, "Sorry." She gave me a nod, and I went over to the bulletin board as if interested in something when, in reality, I contemplated where Ethan would be in the library. Possibly the computer room using the internet since I sincerely doubted he was here to check out a book on something.

"I'll check out these, please." Ethan's deep voice resounded behind me.

I swung around, and there he was, handing Mrs. Kessler two thick hardbound books and one smaller paperback to borrow. Keeping my face pointed toward the bulletin board, I watched him waiting for the librarian to stamp his card. Pretending to read a lost dog flyer, I timed it so that when he reached the door, I was headed there as well.

"Well, fancy meeting you here," I said, cringing at how lame my words sounded.

"Hello." He raised his books for me to see, as if they'd validate his being there. "Believe it or not, I'm an avid reader now that I have so much time on my hands."

"Who's running the shop while you're over here looking for something to read?" I asked.

"I've closed down the ice cream parlor for the time being." Ethan tucked the books under his arm long enough to open the door for us. "No use working until they've finished remodeling."

"Oh, are they going to finally fix it?" I grabbed hold of the handrail. The steps weren't steep, but I had been known to be clumsy from time to time.

"Yeah." He sounded less stressed than when I'd last spoken with him. "Brynn's working with contractors now to set up a schedule."

"Wouldn't it be faster to just find a better location?" I asked and then realized late autumn might be considered a slower season for him, so this wasn't the best time to be making a move.

"Maybe," Ethan said with a shrug and then moved closer to me when a couple going up the steps needed room to pass. "But breaking the contract would leave me penniless." A flash of anger darkened his complexion, but then he smiled and said, "Things may be looking up for me soon."

"How's that?" I asked when we reached the sidewalk.

Ethan stuffed his books under his arm again and peered at an expensive-looking watch on his wrist. "Sorry, I've got to run."

I wanted to press him for more information, but he took off in a hurry. Out of ideas and no longer in the mood to shop, I went home. Still at work, Ava had driven herself to The Park since she knew I'd planned to take off early today. The house was empty, and Cocoa wasn't in her favorite spot in the den. The cat liked to sleep in Ava's chair by the window during this time of day to catch a few rays of sunshine.

"Cocoa?" I checked throughout the house, and when I reached the kitchen, I found her sitting on the windowsill staring outside.

"What's up, girl?" I said while I made sure she had fresh water and food in her princess style kitty dish.

The cat didn't respond, not that I expected her to, but she appeared to be entranced by something in the backyard.

I looked to see what had her attention, expecting a squirrel or bird to be teasing her inability to catch them from inside the house. Someone had left the back gate wide open. The only time we went out there was to drag the trash bins out to the bottom of the driveway on trash day. They'd picked up the trash the day before yesterday, and I'd put the empty rubber bins back myself. I was sure I'd shut the gate, but maybe I hadn't pulled it tight enough.

"Don't worry. I'll take care of it, Cocoa." I ran my hand over her back and scratched behind her ears before heading out the kitchen door.

A cool gust of wind tugged at my hair, reminding me winter would be here before too long. One of the trash cans lay on its side, so I picked it up and then shut the wooden gate. This time, I secured the latch and pulled on it to make sure it held tight. On the ground, there was an unusual mark in the damp soil along the edge of the house. It appeared to be a large shoe print. When I hovered my foot over it, it surprised me to find the shoe size was much bigger than mine. Ava wore a smaller size. A shiver raised on the nape of my neck. Who had been back here? It could have been Jack. Pat might have had him stop by to check up on something as she did from time to time.

When I returned to the kitchen, I opened a can of tuna, drained the juice, and gave it to the cat before I grabbed the mayo from the fridge. After making myself a tuna sandwich loaded with lettuce, onions, and tomatoes, I added a handful of chips to the plate and then went into the den with my food and a can of soda.

I got out the notepad I'd been using to keep track of suspects.

Sam had opportunity and motive. Could he have entered Mr. Rinehart's office demanding compensation, and when the accountant refused, he became so angry he thrashed him on the head with a paperweight? It didn't feel right. Sam was twenty years older and half the size of Melvin.

Sam had been in a hurry to leave when I met him, but he hadn't been out of breath enough to sound winded. He would have had to climb and descend the stairs in between killing a man. I think he would have been short of breath or jittery. He'd been calm, only in a hurry to grab a bite. Besides, the Sam I'd known as a child would never harm anyone.

Next was Ava's good friend, Chloe. Despite my sister's relationship with the suspect, I had to keep an open mind. Chloe had motive if not opportunity. Sam backed up her claim that she hadn't been in the building on Friday morning.

Then came Brynn. The accountant's niece had the most to gain from his death, and she hadn't seemed too upset about his demise. From what I'd learned, she hadn't really known him very well, but still, he had been her father's brother. I liked Brynn. She had such a relaxed yet fun air about her. Friendly and thoughtful, it would have been foolish of her to kill her uncle since he'd been training her to take over the family business, eventually.

Ethan seemed like the one most likely to have done it. Younger, stronger, and angrier than any of the other suspects when it came to Mr. Rinehart's ruthless practices as a landlord. By his own admission, Ethan had no alibi for the time of the murder, and he definitely had motive and means. I wondered what he meant earlier when he told me things might be looking up for him soon. Were he and Brynn getting serious, and if so, had they plotted the murder together?

There was a new name to add, so I wrote Martha Miller on the top of the next page and then turned on my laptop. Since I didn't know much about her, I'd have to rely on social media to give me some clues. After a slow start, I finally found a few interesting tidbits. The accountant's on-again, off-again girlfriend slash cook was forty-five. She and her sister, Louise, relocated to Grady seven years ago from Los Angeles where they both worked for an upscale hotel. Although there was no mention of Mr. Rinehart having any involvement in their decision to move, they'd both started working for him as soon as they hit town. I'd have to toss around some ideas with Ava on this new development next time we discussed the case, but I wasn't in a hurry since there were several photos online dated the day before, on and after Melvin's death, that showed her vacationing in Hawaii with friends.

CHAPTER FOURTEEN
"Home is where the heart is."

————

I took off early on Sunday and went straight home. Since it was Ava's day off, I had a quiet drive alone. Because of our weekend schedules, I hadn't spoken with my sister since Saturday morning. When I left the house earlier in the day, she'd been tutoring one of her online classes in the basement.

"Hi?" I called as soon as I walked into the house. "I'm home."

"Hello. I'm in the kitchen." The singsong note in Ava's voice when she answered reminded me of Mother when we'd return from school. The bittersweet memory took my breath away for a moment. A decade had passed since her death, yet the pain of grief didn't calculate time or space when it struck. I dropped my purse on the couch and forced a smile on my face when I entered the kitchen.

"Pat dropped this casserole off earlier." Ava dished up two plates. "The kids' school activities have her running in circles, so she had to postpone the normal family dinner this week."

"That was sweet of her." My stomach responded to the savory beef and noodles smell with a happy dance.

"Do you mind putting the clothes from the washing machine into the dryer?" Ava pointed in the direction of the laundry room. "While I get the food on the table?"

"Sure." We shared most of the chores, but Ava had a way of getting out of folding clothes almost every time.

"Do you want tea or soda to drink?" she called out.

"Tea is fine." I stuffed damp towels into the dryer, set the timer, and returned to the kitchen. Ava had two glasses of iced tea on the table when I joined her.

"Parker stopped by earlier," she said nonchalantly as she scooted her chair up closer and grabbed her napkin.

"Really?" I stared at her with my mouth open. As far as I knew, Parker had never come by the house before the other night.

He'd dropped her off, but hadn't gone inside. "Did he need something?"

"No, not really," she said with a slight smile and then added, "Well, yes, in a way."

Once I'd grown weary of waiting for her to provide a better answer, I said, "And?"

"His daughter has decided to move in with him next summer," Ava explained.

"Have they met in person yet?" I knew they'd communicated by way of the computer but nothing more.

"No, just on the phone and FaceTime. The two of them are so much alike and get along great." Ava seemed well-informed on the development between Parker and his estranged daughter.

"Wow, that is something." I was surprised, but didn't say so, because I didn't want to upset Ava. It seemed strange that a young woman just out of college would put everything on hold to live with a man who, although he was her biological father, had been a stranger to her not so long ago.

"Yes, it is." Ava beamed with pride, which made me wonder if she had something to do with Parker contacting his daughter in the first place. "She'd like to see about getting a job and settling down here permanently."

I swallowed a bite and then took a sip of my tea before asking, "What's her major?

"She studied journalism and really wants to be a writer." Ava's hint of a smile gave away her attempt to make me think this conversation wasn't planned. "Maybe you could hire her at The Park?"

"I'm not sure, but I'll look into it." Parker was well-liked by The Park owners and the staff, so this little favor seemed like something the bosses would encourage. "We do need a new editor at the newspaper, but I'm not sure…"

"Why?" Ava's eyes grew wide. "It sounds like the perfect thing for her."

"Well." My focus was on the food I was trying to spear with my fork. "We'll have to talk to William's widow first and then there's the committee. They may already have someone in mind for the position."

"You don't have to worry about Betty." One of Ava's best friends from high school was newly widowed and had inherited some property at The Park. The newspaper office was the position her husband had overseen before his death.

"Have her send a resume or have Parker drop one off, and I'll see what I can do."

"I'll let them know." Ava sounded pleased, as if the job for Parker's daughter was a done deal. Before I had time to respond, she changed the subject. "So, do you have any more clues?"

Cocoa came into the kitchen and meowed.

"Feed the cat and I'll go get the notebook," I said as I pushed my chair away from the table. When I returned, both the cat and Ava were happily eating.

I slid into my chair and set the notebook beside my plate. "I did an online search on Martha."

Ava's brows rose with interest. "And what did you find?"

"When Martha and her sister both quit their jobs in L.A.," I explained, "they moved to Grady two weeks later and started working for Mr. Rinehart the next day."

"We know that Martha and the accountant had a thing going on." Ava focused on her drink as she brought her glass of tea to her lips. "Maybe she was jealous of his other women."

Pretending to be mulling over her suggestion, I puckered my lips and then shot down her theory. "I'm pretty sure she didn't do it."

"Why?" The startled look on my sister's face was almost comical.

"I found pictures of her vacationing in Hawaii online." I finally stopped playing and gave her all the facts. "The dates on some of them were at the time of the murder."

Ava rolled her eyes at me and then asked, "So, who does that leave on your list?"

"Brynn," I answered before I opened the notebook. "But she has a strong alibi that shows she was out of town when the murder took place."

"But we haven't ruled her out as a conspirator," Ava reminded me, even though I'd been the one who came up with the accomplice theory first.

"The more I get to know her, the harder it is to believe she would have wanted him dead." Brynn seemed too smart to risk teaming up with someone else to knock off her uncle. "She had access to everything, and he was training her to take over. His death leaves her with more responsibilities she's not ready to handle."

"All right then." Ava put her glass down and nibbled on the corner of her bottom lip before adding, "Ethan could have done it with or without her help."

"Yes," I said because she was exactly right. Ethan had reason and motive all on his own. "Now that the accountant is gone, Ethan is getting what he wanted."

"Do you mean a new shop?" Ava asked with a sly smile. "Or a new girl?"

"Well, I meant shop." It was my turn to roll my eyes. "I'm not sure about the girlfriend part, but I can't imagine Brynn seeing anything in Ethan."

Ava glanced at the clock on the wall and let out a sigh. "Who does that leave us with?"

I flipped the page on my notebook and cringed. My sister wasn't going to like this. "Chloe's next."

"No." Ava waved away the very notion of her friend being involved. "She didn't do it."

"He did her wrong," I reminded her gently. "Maybe worse than all the others. He let her think he had feelings for her, took advantage of her tender heart, and then crushed it."

"Yes, but she's no killer." Ava gave me one of Pat's best *I'm in charge and that's all you need to know* looks that she gave her kids when they got out of line.

Resigned to pursuing that one on my own, I turned to the next page. "Sam's the last one I have on my list."

"Right." Ava frowned. "He had opportunity and motive. I wonder if Jack and Cody consider him as a suspect."

"They haven't said anything to me," I told her, but I planned to find out the next time I spoke with one of them.

"Well, I don't know about you"—Ava paused and let out a yawn—"but I'm going to head on up to bed. It's been a long weekend."

"Good night," I said to her. "I'm going to stay down here and read while I wait for the clothes to dry."

It wasn't until later, when I was in my room, that I'd realized I'd forgotten to mention someone had left the gate open and the footprint I'd discovered.

CHAPTER FIFTEEN
"Look before you leap."

———

Monday morning, I took a seat behind my desk and slipped off my boots one after the other, letting out a sigh of relief each time one of my feet found freedom. The outfit I wore for work was fine except for those tall leather boots. Some days, they were worse than others. The trek up the hill from the parking lot to the main entrance had done a number on my feet this morning. We had the option of riding in on one of the trams scheduled to circle the parking lot every half hour, but I never would have heard the end of it from Ava if I'd taken the easy way out and had opted to catch a ride.

I wiggled my toes and smiled. Hidden under my desk, I wouldn't have to put my feet back into captivity until my first tour scheduled after my lunch break. This morning, I had to go over the time sheets before working on the payroll tomorrow. Coming through the window, I heard the hum of customers milling about. Otherwise, it was quiet inside the building until my phone rang.

"Miss Cranston?" Joyce asked. Hearing her use my last name over the phone could only mean someone she didn't know was standing at the receptionist's desk. "There's a gentleman out here who would like to speak with you."

"Can you ask him his name?" I really wasn't in the mood to see anyone. My workload had nearly doubled with Gretchen away. Joyce filled in answering the phone and taking messages, but I counted on my assistant to do much more than be friendly.

There was a pause on the line as I assumed she was asking their name.

"Sam Smith is here to see you," she said.

Sam? I'd never seen him at The Park before and was surprised to have him stopping by to see me. "I'll be right there."

It took me a few minutes to put my boots back on and set the time sheets I'd been working on in a file before shoving them in a drawer to work on later. Not wanting to make him wait, I hurried out of my office to see what my father's favorite barber needed to see me about.

"Hi, Sam," I said when I entered the lobby. He wore a comfortable brown cashmere sweater over his plaid shirt, which reminded me of something my father would have worn when out visiting friends. "How can I help you?"

His brows creased and he squared his shoulders. "I need to talk with you if you have a few minutes to spare."

"Sure, come on back to my office," I said, surprised by his rigid stance and formal presence. It sounded like he had something serious on his mind.

"Thank you." Sam followed me down the hall and waited for me to enter my office before he stepped over the threshold.

I waved my hand in the direction of the chairs across from my desk. "Have a seat," I said before sitting down myself.

"Thanks." Sam gave me a polite nod as he sat on the visitor's chair closest to the door.

In the dim lobby light, I hadn't realized how red in the face he looked or noticed his heavy breathing. The hike from the parking lot must have been too much for him.

"Would you like something to drink?" I asked, unable to keep the concerned tone from my voice. "We have bottled water and soda."

"No," he waved his hand. "I'm fine. Besides, you're busy and I can't stay long. There's just something I need to say to you."

"All right," I said. Still uneasy about his health, I leaned forward resting my arms on the top of the desk and kept a watchful eye on him while we spoke. "What is it you need to tell me?"

"People are talking about you snooping around town asking a lot of questions," Sam said. The words came out sounding stiff, as if he'd rehearsed them on the way here. "And as a friend of your father's, I think he'd want me to tell you to back off the case before you get hurt."

My shoulder's stiffened, and I pulled my arms back to my sides. Annoyed by what sounded like a warning, I asked, "Is that a threat?"

"No." He shook his head and waved the palm of his hand in front of his torso. "I'm just letting you know as a friend of your family that I'm worried. If you don't stop asking questions, the real killer may feel like he has to do something to silence you."

"He?" I asked, thinking maybe someone had coerced him to come here and give me this strange yet sinister message. "Do you have any idea who the actual killer is?"

"Of course not," Sam said emphatically with his chin raised, and then he stood and gave me a long steady stare before adding, "Just be careful."

Bewildered by his message, I rose and walked around the desk to join him at the door. "I will, I promise."

"Good," he said, without making eye contact with me. "Now, if you'll excuse me, I need to get back to the barber shop."

"Have a nice day." I opened the door and waved him goodbye before I hurried to my desk so I could get Joyce on the line.

"Hello?" she answered.

"Have one of the tram drivers meet Sam at the gate. I don't want him walking all the way to the parking lot," I told her and then added, "And don't let him know we arranged it."

Park employees usually communicated by way of walkie talkies, but the receptionist had the ability to call the tram drivers' vehicles by phone in case of emergencies. Unlike me, Joyce would be able to reach one of them and keep the conversation private.

When I returned to my work on the computer screen, I wondered who Sam meant when he said people were complaining about my snooping around. Why hadn't I thought to ask for names? I mentally kicked myself for not digging deeper for more information. Letting out a sigh, I picked up where I'd left off before Sam's visit by entering data into the employee payroll software program.

My phone rang right before closing time, and I recognized Ava's number. It was strange for her to be calling when we would be seeing each other in about five minutes.

"Hey, what's up?" I put the phone on speaker so I could shut down the computer while we talked.

"Lily," she said. "Don't forget, I'm having dinner with the girls tonight."

At least once a month, Ava and the girls she once worked with when she owned a beauty salon went out to eat. Chloe would be among them, but I doubted Ava would bring up the murder investigation. Still, you never know, she might learn something we would find helpful.

"Thanks for reminding me," I said since I had forgotten. Rising from my desk, I pushed the chair in and glanced at the clock. "I'll see you when you get home."

After we hung up, I gathered my things and turned off the light before I left my office, making sure to lock the door behind me. Joyce was still sitting at the receptionist's desk in the lobby when I entered. She had her hand on the phone but took it off when she saw me. "Hi, I was just about to call you to let you know I was leaving."

"Thanks for all your help today," I said since I appreciated her stepping in when we needed her. "I'll shut off the lights and lock the front door after you go. See you tomorrow."

"All right, then. See you tomorrow." She grabbed her purse and waved goodbye as she left the building.

By myself, it was quiet inside the lobby, but outside, there was still activity going on. The café and saloon both stayed open later than the other attractions and were popular eateries with the locals. My drive home was lonely without Ava, and I had an empty house to look forward to, but there was the new book by my favorite author waiting for me at home. An empty house, a bowl of mixed nuts and something to drink by my side, along with a good book to read, sounded like just the relaxing evening I needed.

I parked the Jeep in the driveway and walked up the steps. It was still light outside, although the sky was cloudy. When I put the key in the lock, I heard a thump on the front windowpane. Cocoa stood on the back of the couch watching me, and when I looked at her, she meowed. At least someone was waiting for me. As soon as I got inside, she came over to where I stood and rubbed her fur against my ankles.

"Good Kitty," I told her, slipped off my shoes, and headed for the kitchen to make sure she had food and water. Once I had her taken care of, I opened the fridge. Since I'd eaten a late lunch, I wasn't very hungry, so I poured myself a glass of iced tea and took it into the den where I'd left the book I wanted to read.

Cocoa darted into the den and jumped into Ava's chair. She looked frazzled.

"What's the matter, girl?" I cooed and reached over to pet her. As much as I loved cats, this one had chosen my sister as her human. "Don't worry. Ava will be home soon."

The cat arched her back and hissed. Surprised by her odd behavior, I glanced over my shoulder, expecting to find a rodent or something the cat would find offensive. Nothing lurked in the corner, and the floor was clear. What had gotten into her? I set my glass on the table beside me and stood. A strange dinging sound came from the basement. Ava had had a class early this morning and must have left her computer on. Strange noises going off all day would explain the cat's anxiety.

"It's okay, Cocoa. Ava must have left something on in her schoolroom," I said to the cat. Either that or she'd forgotten to set the bolt lock on the basement door. Unless it was sealed tight, a strong breeze was all it took to blow it open.

I didn't venture downstairs very often, since it was clearly my sister's domain, but when I heard the strange sound again, I put down my book and decided to go investigate. I gave Cocoa a quick pet on the head and mumbled, "I'll go turn it off."

At the top of the landing, I flipped on the light, and the underground room filled with shadows. My sister's computer and supplies were in the far corner near the entrance to the outside of the house. She had a standing lamp to use when she taught online. I'd be able to see much better once I turned it on. The old wooden stairway creaked with each step I took. We should have someone look at them to have them replaced. When I reached the bottom of the stairs, I sensed movement to the left of me and then something hard came crashing down on the back of my head. I stumbled forward and fell to my knees. Dazed, I sat down, looked up, and caught a glimpse of someone's back as they ran out the exterior basement door.

My phone was upstairs on the coffee table where I'd left it. I needed to call for help, but wasn't sure if the intruder had left the property or circled around to the front of the house. I reached for the railing to pull myself up, but a wave of dizziness washed over me and turned my stomach.

The sound of a car door shutting came from outside and my heart froze. Was the intruder coming back? Footsteps on the pavement grew louder as they approached the basement. I searched for a place to hide, but my head throbbed, and the room was spinning. If I ducked behind the shelves full of boxes, whoever it was might not see me in the dim light. The door creaked as someone pulled it open wider. I froze. There wasn't time to hide.

"Lily?" Cody's voice called from the doorway.

As relief flooded my body, I sank down onto the bottom step and blinked back tears. "I'm over here by the stairs."

Cody stepped into the basement and then hurried across the floor to where I sat. When he reached my side, he sat a bag on the floor and crouched beside me. "Are you okay? What happened?"

Shadows and bad lighting made it hard to read his face, but he sounded concerned.

"Yes." I rubbed the back of my head and felt a knot, which was a good sign because the injury was swelling out and not in. "I'm fine."

Cody took me by the arm and helped me to my feet. "Did you fall down the stairs?" He looked toward the top of the landing as if to gauge the distance.

"No, I heard a noise down here and thought Ava's computer was on," I explained. Still dizzy, the room spun for a moment but soon righted itself. "There was someone else down here, and whoever it was, they hit me on the head with something."

"Here, sit down." Cody glanced up at the dim light bulb overhead and then helped me settle on the second to the last step. It was much more comfortable, so I rested my head on the railing.

"There's a lamp next to Ava's desk that will give us better light," I said and pointed to the other side of the room.

Cody crossed the basement floor and turned on the light. It surprised me to see the mess the intruder had left. I wondered how long they'd been down here and what they expected to find.

"Was there just one person?" Cody morphed into full officer mode. "Did you recognize who it was?"

"I think there was just one person, and all I saw was their back," I said. "If I'd known anyone was down here, I would have stayed upstairs and called the police."

Cody moved to the door, careful not to touch it with his hand. "It doesn't look like they broke in here."

"How did you know I needed help?" I asked.

He'd appeared out of nowhere and had to have been on his way to the house for some other reason. The hit on the head must have been harder than I thought because I'm sure I would have remembered Cody saying he'd be coming over if he had.

"I didn't know anything was wrong," Cody said and then explained. "Ava saw me in town, and she told me you were home alone tonight, so I thought I'd surprise you with Chinese takeout for dinner. When I saw the basement door wide open, I didn't know what was going on."

"I'm sure it was shut when we left for work this morning." I raised my face to look at the ceiling, trying to recall how the house appeared when I'd arrived home. "And I'm sure I would have noticed if it were open when I pulled into the driveway earlier."

"Are you sure you're okay?" Judging by his expression, I must have said something strange.

"Yes, I'm fine." When I started to stand, Cody helped me up and put his hand on my back, and before I knew it, he'd scooped me up and carried me to the top of the staircase.

Being held in his muscular arms was everything I ever dreamed it would be. My heart raced, and a tingling sensation ran through my veins. But it was a bit awkward to be treated like an invalid. I could have walked up the stairs myself, but who was I to complain?

"Someone must have been in the house when I got home and snuck down into the basement before I entered the house," I told Cody when he sat me down on the couch in the living room. It was the only thing that made sense. Or they could have been in the basement the whole time, but again, why?

"Was the front door locked?" Cody asked as he went through each room on the first floor.

"Yes, I remember taking out my keys and unlocking the door when I got home," I said, speaking loud enough for him to hear from the dining room. "I guess they could have locked the door behind them."

"I found out how they got in." Cody's call came from the kitchen, so I followed the sound of his voice. He stood at the sink and pointed out a footprint on the counter. The window above the basin was raised slightly.

"I don't know how I missed that when I got myself a glass of iced tea earlier." I looked around the room, and everything else looked fine. At least the burglar had been neat during his search.

"They couldn't have been very tall," Cody said, looking closer but careful not to touch anything.

Once Cody was sure no one was hiding on the main floor, he motioned for me to sit on the couch while he checked upstairs. My stomach rumbled while I waited, and my thoughts went to the bag Cody left in the basement. Was that the Chinese food he'd spoken of earlier?

"It doesn't look like anything is missing," he said to someone on his phone while coming back down the stairs. "I'll have Lily check to make sure."

Cody ended the call and pocketed his phone. "Jack's sending a team over to check for prints."

"There's nothing missing that I can see," I told him after I'd looked around the house myself. "But I'll have Ava check as well when she gets home."

In the den, I found the glass of tea I had left on the table. The ice had melted, and it was watered down, so I took it into the kitchen. After all the excitement, I needed something stronger.

"Would you like anything to drink?" I raised my voice while standing in front of the sink, where I'd poured out the diluted tea.

"Sure." Apparently, Cody had followed me into the kitchen. The sound of his voice was so close that I jumped and let out a gasp.

"Are you okay?" he asked again with a look of concern on his face as he placed his hand on my arm.

"Yes, I'm fine," I told him. "Just a little jumpy. There are some sodas in the fridge. Help yourself."

Cody pulled out two cans, set them on the counter, and opened them before sliding one closer to me. When I looked out the window above the basin, I remembered how someone had left the back gate open the other day.

"I wonder if it was the same person from before," I said, speaking my thoughts aloud.

Cody looked at me, eyebrows raised. "What are you talking about? Was someone here before?"

"I'm not sure." As I told him about the gate being left open, and the footprint I'd found, Cody set down his drink and got up to go outside to investigate.

"We'll want to compare the footprints from under the window with those by the gate," he said and then asked me to stay inside, so I moved to the sink where I could watch him from the window.

While he was looking at the lock on the gate, Jack pulled up in his car with a C.S.I van right behind him. Jack let his team of investigators in through the outside basement door before he climbed up to the main floor.

"Lily?" He called out my name and found me in the kitchen as Cody returned from the backyard. "Everything okay in here?"

"Yes. I think so," I said, suddenly wishing I could turn back the clock and start this day over again. From now on, I planned to make sure all the doors were locked tight when I left the house.

Cody filled Jack in on what he'd discovered and suggested the crime scene team start in the basement and outside the kitchen window before coming upstairs.

"Let's have a seat." Cody nodded in the direction of the table.

"Jack, would you like something to drink?" I asked. Ava would have been pleased to know I remembered my hostess skills.

"No, I'm fine," he said, so we all sat down at the table, where I filled Jack in on what had happened. He seemed surprised to hear nothing had been taken. Not that we left a lot of valuables lying around the house, but it did seem odd for someone to break in just to look around.

"I wonder what he was looking for since it doesn't appear to have been a robbery." Jack crossed his arms and narrowed his eyes the way he did when brewing over something.

"Well…" I kept my voice even and calm, knowing I was about to open a can of worms. "Do you think it might have something to do with my being framed for embezzlement or the murder of the man who'd been investigating me?"

Wrapped up in their murder case and without The Park owners opening a criminal investigation, my little problem of fighting to prove I wasn't an embezzler seemed to have fallen under their radar. Jack lowered his arms and, raising his brows, frowned at me. I suddenly wished I'd kept my mouth shut. Cody ducked his chin and bit down on his bottom lip.

Traitor.

"Lily, please tell me you haven't been doing any amateur investigating again?" His less than subtle reference to my unprofessional attempt last summer to help a friend clear their name hit the mark. I felt bad for all the trouble I'd caused, but it had all worked out for the best in the end.

"I can't help believing the murder and the missing money are related." There was no doubt in my mind, and once they took me seriously, they would make progress on finding the killer.

"Okay, start from the beginning." Jack's eyes looked weary, and he heaved a heavy sigh.

"Well to start with, did you know Mr. Rinehart was an awful landlord?" I glanced from Jack to Cody, but neither of their expressions gave me a clue if they knew this to be true.

"Go on," Jack urged, and then he glanced at the watch on his arm.

"Poor Sam Smith, he should have had enough money saved to retire," I said, ignoring my brother-in-law's indifference. "But the accountant tricked him into giving up his prime location on Main Street to move into the new complex."

"How did he trick him?" Cody looked doubtful.

"He told Sam business would be better on the east end of town," I explained before pausing to take a sip of soda. "But as soon as Sam moved out, Mr. Rinehart rented his old building to a family haircutting salon, and they've taken all of Sam's business."

"I've been to Family Hair Cuts," Jack said with a slight shrug. "And the problem may not all be about location. They're good, they're fast, and the prices are reasonable."

"Okay, so maybe I let nostalgia and loyalty cloud my vision," I said, still believing Sam had been cheated. "But I'm sure you know Sam's not the only tenant with a complaint."

"Who else have you spoken with?" Jack rose from the table and opened the fridge.

Cody sat silently, sipping his soda when a wayward strand of hair fell across his brow. He brushed it back, and I decided the next time we were alone I'd try to get him to visit Sam's place.

"Ethan Pierce can't sell ice cream because the accountant wouldn't fix his freezer." I twisted my torso and watched Jack pull out a can of soda before he returned to the table. "How can the man be expected to pay child support without making any money?"

"I'm aware of Ethan's issues." Jack returned to the table with his drink. "Killing Mr. Rinehart wouldn't have helped his situation any."

"All right then, there's Chloe. Her salon is squeezed into a tiny shop." I felt guilty for throwing Ava's friend's name into the mix, but since we were discussing disgruntled renters, she made the list. "Mr. Rinehart promised her a deluxe office space upstairs but dumped her as his girlfriend right after she signed the lease."

"Can you explain how any of these 'suggestions' fit in with your being falsely accused of a crime?" Jack didn't sound impressed with any of my theories.

"No, but don't you see, that's just the thing?" I threw my hands up in exasperation. "If I could find the connection, I'm positive it would solve both cases."

Jack looked at Cody and raised one brow. Then he shifted his eyes to pin me with his famous no-more-nonsense gaze. "All I see is you need to back off the case, Lily, before you cross the wrong person."

"There is one thing I can tell you." Cody reached out and laid his hand on top of mine. "We have spoken with all the people on your list, and none of them is a suspect at this time."

"None?" I found his statement hard to believe.

Jack rose from the table and went to check on the crime scene. My stomach rumbled and Cody smiled, looked around, and then said, "I'll be right back."

It didn't take him long to return with the Chinese takeout he'd left in the basement earlier in the evening when he'd come to my rescue. I started to heat plates for both of us, but he had to get back to work.

"Enjoy your food," he said with a look of sympathy before heading back to the basement. I must have looked as discouraged as I felt.

When I'd finished, I went into the den and picked up the mystery I'd started reading earlier in the evening, ignoring the activity going on around me. Sometimes a good book is all it took to escape the reality of a bad situation.

"I doubt the intruder will be back," Jack informed me after his team had dusted for prints. "But I will have a patrol car drive by throughout the night."

"Okay." I walked him to the front door pretty sure I'd be getting a call from Pat soon. "Thanks."

"Lily." My brother-in-law put his hand on my shoulder. "I don't want you to get hurt. Please be careful and keep me or Cody in the loop."

"All right," I promised, but my discouragement and frustration made it hard for me to make eye contact with him.

"The basement door is fixed and locked tight." He glanced toward the kitchen. "We've secured all the entrance doors and windows."

"I'll be sure to lock this door too." His concern for my safety was evident, so I smiled to reassure him. "Don't worry, Ava will be home soon, and I know who to call if we need anything."

I was glad he wasn't going to have an officer parked out front like last summer. They had work to do, and we didn't need a babysitter. Thankfully, Ava didn't return home until after the C.S.I.

van had left. She would hate that she missed all the excitement. Better she had a quiet evening with her friends instead of worrying about who or what might be lurking in the corners.

Later, while trying to fall asleep, my mind centered on reasons why someone would break into our home. We didn't have anything of real value, but burglars broke into houses every day. Anyone might consider the secluded farmhouse a good place to snoop. But by all appearances, today hadn't been their first visit. What were they looking for?

The cufflink!

I sat up in bed and turned on the lamp beside me. That had to be the reason. But how did they know I was the one who had picked it up? Sighing inwardly, I made a mental note to mention my concerns to Cody the next time I saw him. Yes, I'd found it on the day of the murder but not anywhere near the crime scene. He was sure to think I was grasping at straws. I looked at the clock. It was after midnight, so I flopped back down, fixed my pillow, and squeezed my eyes shut, willing my mind to shut down and let me rest.

CHAPTER SIXTEEN
"Never judge a book by its cover."

———

Exhausted from the events of the night before, I had to drag myself into work on Tuesday. After being knocked down in the dark by an intruder in my house then grilled by my brother-in-law and possible boyfriend over the investigation, I'd had a hard time trying to fall asleep. To make matters worse, it was my day to do payroll, so somehow, I had to stay focused.

Joyce buzzed my phone at half past nine to let me know I had a call.

"Do you know who it is?" I don't always ask, but I had been procrastinating from doing payroll by typing a reply to a question on The Park's web page. Gretchen knew to field all my calls on Tuesday.

"It's Brynn Rinehart," Joyce informed me. So of course, out of curiosity, I had to take the call.

"Hello," I said once Joyce had transferred Brynn. "Lily Cranston speaking."

"Hi, Lily. I'm sorry to bother you at work." Brynn sounded hesitant, as if she were trying to convince herself it was all right to speak with me which came as a surprise, considering the confidence that had oozed from her during our previous encounters. "But I was wondering if you'd be able to meet me for lunch today. My treat."

After Saturday's break-in, I was wary of being alone with anyone from the suspect list but still interested to know why she wanted to meet for lunch.

"Well." I gave in without much of a fight. "It will have to be quick. I have a lot of work today."

"Great." She sounded pleased by my response. "How about the China Garden House at noon?"

"That sounds good." I loved their lunch buffet so much I didn't mind going there, even though I'd had Chinese food last night. Four long counters filled with a wide variety of delicious Chinese dishes lined the center of the restaurant. Divided so the warm cuisine stayed steamy hot and the cold food chilled, eating there was a pleasant experience but best to go when hungry.

"Great," she said. "I'll stop by and pick you up."

"Oh no, that's not necessary," I insisted. Why would she drive from town to The Park when we were going to eat in town? "The Park is too far out of your way. Besides, I have the Jeep."

"I'll be coming from the direction of the trailer park on Old Quarry Road," Brynn said. "See you at noon."

She hung up without waiting for my reply. I wondered if she'd considered the fact that she would have to drive me back to work.

I had a meeting with the groundskeeping department coming up at ten, so I finished reading emails and left the office early to take a walk around the compound. Payroll could wait until after lunch. I enjoyed getting out and seeing groups of people experiencing life in the late 1800s. The amazement on their faces lifted my spirits, and that's exactly what I needed at the moment.

I strolled down Main Street until I came to the corner. On my right was the entrance to the assay office. The station was set up to recreate the experience gold diggers had when checking on their ore samples. Derrick Best, a real-life retired assayer, did a wonderful job of explaining what was involved in proofing gold. On the other side of the street to the left was the road that led to the mine. I crossed the road and traveled back in the direction of the office instead of hiking up the hill to the mine.

On the east side of town now, I passed the saloon, bank, and sheriff's office where most of the shows took place. Farther up I came to the photo shop, but Lauren had hung out the closed sign, so I didn't bother going in. When I returned to the office, I stopped by the receptionist's desk and spoke with Joyce. "Any messages for me?"

"No." Her smile went from polite to playful. "Did you have a nice chat with Miss Rinehart earlier?"

Unsure of her meaning, I shrugged and said, "She asked me to meet her for lunch today."

"Oh." Joyce's expression dropped. "I don't think that's a good idea."

"Why?" I asked, curious as to how Joyce even knew Brynn.

"She has a reputation for scamming people," Joyce said to my surprise.

"Really?" Of course, I wanted to know more. Any lead that took me closer to solving the case was good. "Have you met Brynn?"

"I met her at the craft show on Main Street last summer," Joyce explained. "We were both browsing the turquoise jewelry booth when we bumped into each other. She's very friendly, and we got to talking and ended up chatting for a while."

Her description fit Brynn to a tee, but I had to ask, "And she told you she scammed people for fun?"

"No, when I got home, I searched for her on social media thinking we could be friends," Joyce said with a hint of a giggle and then pecked away on her keyboard searching for something online. "Let me show you. I found out she'd been sentenced to three years' probation for being part of an online group attempting to cheat elderly people out of money."

It took her a few minutes to find what she was looking for. Finally, Joyce pulled up a news feed from six years ago. I dragged a chair closer to sit beside her and read the article. According to The Dallas Star Online News Journal, a group of college students were found guilty of senior fraud. They'd contact newly widowed senior citizens about purchases their spouse made prior to death that needed to be paid off. Although their claims sounded plausible, there weren't any such items on layaway. The whole scheme sounded heartless and cruel to stir a grieving person's pain for personal gain.

"That's terrible," I whispered in disbelief. Who in their right mind would stoop so low for any amount of money?

Joyce nodded in agreement. "She moved to Grady after serving her sentence."

"Can you forward the link to me?" I asked since I wanted to take a closer look.

Alone at my desk, I pulled up all the information possible on the crime Brynn had supposedly been convicted of. From what Joyce told me, Brynn's sentence had seemed lenient for the offense. Once I'd read more details, it made more sense. Brynn had not actually taken part in scamming the elderly, although she'd provided information the group of scoundrels used. In her defense, she said she hadn't known it was a con. She believed their story when they told her they had something purchased by the deceased that would be a blessing to the grieving spouses.

Had I found out otherwise, I would have canceled our luncheon date. The meeting with the groundskeepers took less than an hour, so it gave me time to finish a few emails before I had to get ready to leave for lunch. I updated Joyce on my findings regarding Brynn and then made sure she knew where I was going to be in case something happened.

Brynn showed up at my office ten minutes before twelve. "Your lunch date is here," Joyce said when I answered her call.

"Thanks," I told her. "I'll be right out." After I shut down my computer, I entered the lobby where I found Brynn chatting with Joyce. The accountant's niece must have been a fan of dusters because the one she wore this time was light pink with a rainbow of pastel colors along the neck, bottom and on the cuffs of the sleeves. The light sheer material covered a classy tan pantsuit. Her accessories included a turquoise necklace and matching earrings.

She and Joyce were talking like old friends. Their conversation seemed pleasant enough, which surprised me after my earlier conversation with Joyce. The tension I'd expected there to be between the two of them wasn't evident. Did Brynn have any idea Joyce had looked into her past?

The red convertible Brynn liked to ride around town in was parked close to the entrance, and she'd left the top down. It was a nice day for a drive, and I was looking forward to the ride. There were no clouds in the sky, and a gentle breeze blew in from the west. It seemed sort of silly for Brynn to drive me all the way back to The Park when I could have followed her in the Jeep, but who was I to argue?

I was curious as to why she'd been out on Old Quarry Road, so I asked, "Can you believe I was born and raised in Grady but never knew there was a trailer park out by the old quarry?"

"From what I know, it hasn't been there long." Brynn climbed into the car and waited for me to buckle. "My uncle owned the property, and he turned it into a trailer park. It's quite nice, actually. Each of the lots have their own shade trees and private access to the river with a dock. Since it's a retirement community, most of the tenants are in their mid-sixties and easy to deal with."

How interesting. Talk about not putting all your eggs in one basket. The accountant had been a busy investor. Brynn continued talking, "I appreciate your willingness to meet with me on such short notice."

"Chinese food is one of my favorites." The China Garden was the only Chinese restaurant in Grady. My sisters and I went there on special occasions because they served delicious buffet style food which made it easy to overeat.

I put on my shades and let the wind blow in my hair as we drove to town. Brynn turned on the radio, and we traveled in style. Kicking back and relaxing to the music, I was surprised when Brynn turned right at the railroad tracks instead of continuing straight ahead to the restaurant.

"I hope you don't mind if we take a short detour," she said with a grin. The shades she wore made it impossible to tell what was behind her smile. "I need to drop something off at the warehouse."

Warehouse? I had no idea where she was taking me. After crossing the tracks, we turned left on a service road with tall timbers on either side. There weren't any houses or buildings in sight. At the memory of last night's break-in and the news article this morning, my inner core stiffened. Lulled by the music and fancy ride, I'd let down my guard.

Brynn turned right onto a gravel road that went on for a few hundred yards before the tree-lined path gave way to a large, worn-out looking building. Above the big overhead door, there was a sign that read Grady Welding Shop. I'd forgotten this place was even out here.

"I promised the guys I'd drop off this new torch tip." She put the car in park and removed her sunglasses. "They've been cutting out old machinery rails to remodel and renovate the place. All the work has worn out their torch tips."

"Oh," I said as if I understood what she was talking about.

Brynn grabbed her purse and pulled out a small package. "I'll be right back."

I let out a breath of relief and laughed at myself for being so paranoid. I felt even sillier when Tod, the younger brother of one of our employees, met Brynn at the door. Just out of high school, the young man glanced in my direction and waved.

Once we were back on the road, it didn't take long to reach the restaurant. Inside, our friendly server, who identified herself as Grace, welcomed us and then led the way to a table by the front window. After we'd taken our seats, she took our drink orders and told us to help ourselves at the buffet. As I perused the rows of scrumptious looking dishes, I piled my plate with sesame seed chicken, fried rice, hot pots, and green beans. Our glasses of tea were waiting at the table when we returned.

"The food is so good here," Brynn said when she sat down across from me, although her plate appeared sparse with only broccoli and fried rice. I mentally shrugged it off since some people liked to make several trips at a buffet.

"Yes, I agree." I stabbed some sesame chicken with my fork and said, "It's one of my family's favorite places to eat."

"Thank you for agreeing to meet with me on such short notice," she said after taking a sip of her drink. "I wanted to see you because I believe you have something I need."

"Oh?" I half expected her to ask for the cufflink, but instead she said, "You have experience and knowledge I could really use right about now. Besides wanting to be friends, I asked you to lunch because I'll be taking over running my uncle's rental spaces and have no idea how to start. I mean, he had started showing me the ropes before he died, but I'm nowhere near ready to take over."

She sounded a bit panicked with good reason. The woman was in over her head. I touched on a few of the basics about running a business during the short amount of time we had. She really needed to take a few college courses if she wanted to succeed. I offered her a few tips and suggested reading material I'd used in school, most of which could be found online.

"You can always call me if you have a question," I offered because I got the feeling Brynn was a lonely person who needed friends. The more time I spent with her the more I liked her. I really hoped she wasn't a murderer.

After lunch, I returned to work and assured Joyce I hadn't been scammed as we'd split the bill, even though Brynn had offered to buy. A few minutes before closing time, my phone rang, and I recognized Steve's number.

Finally. An update on Gretchen's employment status at The Park.

"Hello," I answered in a cautious tone.

"Lilly, this is Steve," he said.

"Yes, hi." Of course, he was Steve. I kept calm, although it felt like the jury was back after a long time deliberating over a high-profile case. I was anxious to hear the verdict.

"We wanted to let you know the team has decided to reinstate Gretchen Thompson," he informed me. I was relieved to hear she would still be working with us but still surprised. Her bubbly personality drew people to her, and the woman was well-liked, but she had committed a crime. Other than my family and the committee, no one knew about her temporary suspension.

"There are conditions she must follow," Steve added with a stern tone in his voice. "Or we'll have to let her go."

"All right." I found myself holding my breath as I waited for him to continue.

"First, she is not allowed access to the petty cash funds or any other of our company's business accounts." Steve's words left no room for argument, which he wouldn't get from me. "We'll need you to take over that part of the job."

"Of course, I understand." I agreed to the extra work, filing it away in my brain for the next time we negotiated a raise in pay.

"And second," he continued. "She must attend weekly therapy sessions to deal with her issues. We've given her the rest of the week off with pay as she had vacation time coming."

Steve could be very fair and kind when he wanted.

CHAPTER SEVENTEEN
"Cry Wolf."

———

The next morning, I arrived at the office before Joyce, which wasn't unusual, but it still felt odd since Gretchen had made a point of being the first one to get to work. Joyce, on the other hand, showed up on time but had a more laid-back personality. She was a good employee who rarely missed work and called if she were going to be late or unable to come in. Still, I missed my friend Gretchen. Her vibrant personality had been something to look forward to when coming into work.

Although right now, it was kind of nice to have the place to myself if only for a few minutes. I turned on the lights and headed for my office, where I sat down in front of my computer and pulled up the notes I'd been keeping on the suspects. After having lunch with Brynn yesterday, I felt sure Ethan was the one most likely to have killed Melvin. But none of that solved the mystery of the larger amount of missing money. Who had been trying to frame me and why?

While reading the website comments posted overnight, my phone rang. I recognized Gretchen's number, which surprised me since we hadn't spoken since her confession. It wasn't that I hadn't wanted to talk to her. It had just felt awkward, like crossing an invisible line that shouldn't be touched until we'd found out the committee's decision. I answered on the third ring, but no one was there.

Worried she'd think I was ignoring her, I called her right back, but the number went to voicemail. That was strange. I pulled up her file and found her home number, but before I had time to dial, my phone buzzed indicating a text message from her.

Sorry, I'm having phone trouble. My car broke down out by The Grove on Old Quarry Road. The tow truck won't be here for another hour, and it's too far to walk anywhere. Can you come get me?

The Grove was a deserted, wooded stretch of land used by hikers and teenagers in the summer. What was she doing there? The only thing out that way was the new trailer park community Cody had told me about the night we sat out on the swing. I replied that I was on my way and could give her a ride to The Park.

Before I locked up the office, I left a note for Joyce telling her I had to run an errand and would be back soon. Still early, a few of the actors were headed for their stations, and guests were starting to arrive. When I reached the parking lot, I climbed into the Jeep and started the engine just as Joyce pulled into the parking lot. She didn't see me, but I felt better knowing the office was being cared for while I was away.

It took a good ten minutes for me to reach The Grove. A long winding dirt road, there weren't any other cars in sight. A few miles longer, but much straighter, most people used the newer paved route when traveling out this way.

I spotted Gretchen's car parked on the side of the road where a patch of ground had been cleared off, right next to a wooded area with a bunch of tall timbers. When I pulled the Jeep next to her vehicle, I spotted Gretchen in the passenger seat of her car. It seemed odd at first, but I supposed since she had a long wait, she'd decided to make herself comfortable. When Gretchen stepped out of the car, there was a look of distress on her face. It was good to see her again, although her clothes surprised me. The pair of old jeans and a baggy sweatshirt she wore gave the appearance of someone down on their luck. My heart went out to her, and I hopped out of the Jeep.

"I'm sorry, Lily." Tears flooded Gretchen's eyes, but before she had time to say another word, her brother, Robert, came around to the passenger side of my vehicle. He must have slipped out from behind the trees where he had to have been hiding.

When Robert raised his hand, my heart sped, and I had a sinking feeling in the pit of my stomach. He held a gun.

"What's going on?" I asked innocently. Apparently, the shock of the situation had dulled my senses.

"You'll see soon enough." Robert raised the weapon and pointed the gun at me. "Stop talking and start walking."

"What are you doing?" I asked. Was he stealing the Jeep because his sister's car was broken down, and he needed wheels? "What's going on? You can take my vehicle if you want."

"You know, for someone who's supposed to be so smart, you aren't too bright." Robert's evil laugh sent a cold shudder down my back.

"Are you the one who killed Mr. Rinehart?" It came out sounding more like a statement than a question, but the grin on his face confirmed the answer was yes.

Ava was never going to believe it when I told her Robert was the killer. If I ever got to tell her. The guy wasn't even on our list of suspects. He'd seemed like a quiet, nice guy, not someone capable of such a heinous crime. Even harder to understand was why he had murdered the accountant. The man had dated his sister once a few years ago, but from all accounts, the breakup was amicable, and they were still on friendly terms. And then there was Gretchen. What did she have to do with all this? My mouth dropped open, and I sent a brief glance in Gretchen's direction.

"I'm so sorry, Lily." Gretchen wrung her hands. Her eyes darted toward the road and then at the two vehicles, as if she were looking for a way to escape. "This is all my fault."

"You're the one who killed Mr. Rinehart?" I gasped. How could Ava and I have been so wrong?

"No, of course not." Her shoulders rose, her brows creased, and then she blinked several times before continuing. "What I meant was it's my fault my brother took money from The Park's account and then tried to frame you."

I was speechless. The whole situation kept getting stranger and stranger. Her brother didn't have access to the bank account. Confusion and betrayal must have registered on my face because Gretchen looked away in shame.

"You see," she took a deep breath and explained, "last summer I saw a pair of earrings I just had to have. They were on sale, but the sale ended the day before my next payday."

Gretchen must have hit her head on something. Her babbling sounded like nonsense, and I had no idea what she was talking about. She'd already confessed to dipping into the petty cash account.

"I had the petty cash fund up on my computer paying bills and thought, *Why not*?" She continued, "Like the other times, I figured no one would know if I borrowed a little to pay for the jewelry. I replaced the money on payday, and no one was the wiser."

Gretchen glared at her brother and then continued, "Except Robert was in town, and he found out. He knew I had a compulsive shopping addiction. I've had it most of my life. Anyhow, I told him how I had been 'borrowing' money from The Park. I needed to get it off my chest, you know? The guilt was keeping me awake at night."

"If the previous manager helped you cover your tracks, how did you get away with it after she left?" I asked while keeping my focus on Robert and his gun. He seemed to be enjoying this moment of truth exchange.

"She told me the only time anyone monitored the account was when sales tax came due, so I'd always be able to plan and cover the extra expenditure."

That explained why Susan Kingsbury hadn't lasted long as a manager for The Park, what with her unscrupulous handling of things. She may not have known it, but she'd opened the door for Gretchen to sink under the spell of her addiction by becoming her enabler. I still didn't see how I fit into all of this.

"What does this have to do with me?" I asked.

"The manager back then didn't pay much attention to detail." Robert rolled his eyes and motioned for us to keep walking. "When they hired you, Gretchen bragged about how much better you were at managing things."

"When I made the mistake of telling my brother about what I had done, he took advantage of it and my position at work." Gretchen sniffed and wiped a tear from her cheek. "Over a month ago, Robert came to me asking for a loan to pay off some men he owed money. When I told him I didn't have any to spare, he reminded me of the times I'd borrowed cash without anyone knowing, but of course, I told him no."

I glanced at her brother, who didn't appear to be concerned that his sister was disclosing information about his theft. That's when I realized the seriousness of the situation and began to doubt I was meant to get out alive. Of course, I should have come to that conclusion when he confessed to the murder, but reality was having a hard time sinking into my confused brain.

"The amount he needed was too big to slip through unnoticed," Gretchen continued. "And besides, I still felt guilty about the times I had done it before."

This overload of information made my head feel tired. "So, how did he get the money?"

Robert laughed. "When she was in the lady's room, I got behind her desk where I'd seen her taking money out of the little safe under there. I also knew where she kept the keys."

"When did all this happen?" I asked as I began to piece the puzzle together.

"In September," he said, this time replacing the irritating laughter with a singsong voice filled with sarcasm. "We were on our way out of town, but Gretchen insisted she wanted me to meet her wonderful new boss first."

"But I didn't meet you until just the other day," I said, although he was right about the money being removed from the accounts back in September, which was over a month ago.

"Nope." He gave me a small, sickening grin, and I recoiled at the mean-spirited man's glare. Robert was a person capable of anything. "You were too busy working to even notice we'd stopped by."

"You'd had several tours booked in a row that day. Joyce was filling in while I was on vacation," Gretchen reminded me. "It wasn't until recently that I learned about the money he'd taken."

Just the other day, she'd come back from lunch with her brother and had looked so upset. How hard it must have been for her to keep up a strong front when she knew Robert was responsible for all the grief I'd had to go through.

"I felt sick when I realized they suspected you, Lily," Gretchen said sorrowfully. "I didn't know what to do. I told my brother that Melvin would eventually trace the missing money right back to me."

"Yeah, I couldn't let my sister lose her job. She had a good racket going on, and I had plans to milk it for all it was worth, so I killed the old geezer," the man said calmly as if he were talking about the weather. "I walked right into his office, and when he asked what I wanted, I grabbed the first thing I saw and knocked him over the head. He never knew what hit him."

"What time was that?" I might as well get all the answers I'd been looking for.

"Right before lunch. You didn't see me, but I was turning out of the parking lot when you pulled in with your Jeep." He motioned for me to keep walking. "If you'd gotten there any sooner, you'd have had a front row seat."

How did Gretchen not know her brother was such a heartless person? She walked on his other side a few feet ahead of us. I didn't recall ever having been in these woods before and had no idea what lay ahead. All I knew for sure was I needed time to find a way out of this situation.

"Does that mean the cufflink belonged to you?" I asked mainly to keep him talking, although it didn't make a lot of sense that the item belonged to him. Why would a golf course maintenance worker need a fancy emblem on his uniform?

"Yeah, I used to work at that casino a long time ago. I like to collect things from places I've been." He raised his arm for me to see the wristwatch he wore, and my stomach turned sour. The time piece looked a lot like the watch my mother bought for my dad years ago. The gold trim around the base stood out against the silver band. "When I saw you showing the cufflink to my sister, I knew I had to get it back, or else they would be able to connect me to the scene of the crime."

"What are you talking about?" Gretchen's face twisted with confusion.

Robert gave his sister a fleeting glance. "A cufflink fell off my shirt when I was leaving Melvin's office building. Miss Nosey over here found it and held on to it."

It was all starting to fall into place now. "So, you're the one who broke into my house."

"Right." He nodded. "Only you came home sooner than I'd expected."

"And then you hit me over the head." I was lucky to be alive, however long that would last.

"You could have killed her, Robert." Gretchen sounded angrier than I'd ever heard her sound before.

"How was I to know her head was so hard?" He rolled his eyes. "She wasn't meant to live. I would have finished her off if her cop boyfriend hadn't showed up."

"But why?" I asked, wondering how Gretchen could be related to someone so evil.

"You are one nosy broad," he said. "I had to do something to shut you up."

"Jack won't stop looking until he finds you," I warned him.

"Not likely," he scoffed. "I typed a suicide note and left it in your Jeep. You couldn't bear the shame of embezzlement which led you to murder Melvin."

"My family would never fall for it," I snapped at him and then shot Gretchen a look of disbelief. "So, your text was a setup."

"The message wasn't from me." She shook her head adamantly. "Robert drove me out here and took my phone. I had no idea what he was up to until it was too late. He's the one who texted you for a ride, pretending to be me."

"Which reminds me." Robert held out his palm.

I stared blankly, feigning confusion and hoping he wasn't asking for my phone. "What?"

"Hand over your phone." His lips curled like a rabid dog. Feeling real fear for the first time since I started this journey, I gave him my cell.

"It's working out just as I planned." His gleeful laugh filled me with dread. How could he go from one extreme to the other in the blink of an eye?

"You must have spent a lot of time putting this all together," I said with sarcasm.

"How else was I ever going to get a chance to kill you?"

"Killing me won't change anything." Panic set in and I looked around, searching for a way to escape. Even if I tried to run, he had a gun. My only hope was to keep him talking. "So how were you able to take money without your sister knowing?"

"Like I told you, I knew about Gretchen's problem. She can't help but buy things she doesn't need. When she told me about her taking money and putting it back, I was impressed. But when she refused to help me pay off this newest gambling debt, I used her key to open the safe and took out the cash. Unfortunately, the bank discovered the missing money before I had time to return it to the safe."

"We never keep that much money in petty cash." I spoke my thoughts aloud.

"It was when we were collecting donations for the new road sign," Gretchen reminded me. "Remember, we kept the checks and cash people dropped off in the safe until you could run by the bank to make a deposit."

"I couldn't believe my luck when they started looking at you instead of her." Robert laughed in my face, and the smell of his bad breath made my eyes water.

Gretchen pulled a tissue from her pocket and blew her nose.

"When my sister found out what I did, she told me Melvin would eventually figure out the connection between the money and the petty cash. He would assume it was her doing since they'd dated before, and he knew about her addiction."

I looked at Gretchen in disbelief. "So, you had your brother kill Mr. Rinehart?"

"No, of course not," Gretchen wailed.

"Without her knowing, I killed the accountant to cover everything up," Robert said without any sign of remorse. The scrawny face and wispy blond hair that had once given him a boyish look now only added to the creepiness of his sinister laugh. "I should have been able to quietly leave town, but no, you had to find the cufflink I'd lost. Still, all I had to do was make it look like you couldn't stand the thought of being discovered and decided to kill yourself."

"None of my friends or family would believe I'd typed such a note," I snapped with irritation. My boots were rubbing blisters on my feet, and by all appearances, I was a goner. Tears filled my eyes, but I quickly blinked them away.

"Is there anything else you'd like to know?" he asked and then added, "Before it's too late?"

Desperate to keep stalling, I asked, "Yes, who is Bob Tomson?"

There was no sign of recognition on Robert's face.

"I don't have a clue," he sneered. "Come on, let's go. Keep walking. You're just trying to get more time."

"No, I'm serious," I said. "In the computer files, there's a suspicious looking employee account with that name on it."

"Wait." Gretchen paused, causing Robert and I to halt our steps as well. "That's the name Susan used for the employee dummy account. Bob Tomson lived in the original town of Calico Rock and was a distant relative of hers, a great-great-grandfather or uncle. I'm not sure which. He's buried out in the cemetery."

"What about the money that went into the account?" I shot a glance at Robert, who seemed interested in hearing the answer as well.

"Susan had us make up a fake employee account for a test run when they put in the new program," Gretchen explained. "She ran a couple small payments through it. I don't know what she did with the money."

"Two small consecutive checks but then a larger one made a year later," I corrected her.

Gretchen's face fell, and she wiped the palm of her hand across her cheek. "I put it back, I promise."

"But Gretchen, you said the petty cash was the only money you'd touched," I reminded her, feeling disappointed.

"Robert got into some trouble with a bookie, and if he didn't come up with some money he said they'd hurt him bad." The look of utter despair on her face made me feel sorry for her.

"Did Susan know about it?" I asked, although I already knew the answer.

"Yes," Gretchen said. "And she can verify I paid it back. It was just a one-time thing."

"What are you so worked up about, Sis?" Robert snorted. "Lily won't be around to squeal on you, and I've got plans for that secret employee account. I think he's due for a raise, and back pay, too."

He motioned with the gun for us to start moving. We walked deeper into the woods, where overgrown foliage and unpruned trees hindered our ability to walk very fast. The farther away we got from the road, the worse my chances were of coming out of the woods alive, so I pretended to trip and fell to my knees. Robert lowered his gun, aiming the business end at my head. I leaned to the side, grabbed a large branch, and used all my strength to whack him on the arm. He dropped the handgun and let out an angry roar. I threw myself flat on the ground and reached for the weapon, but Gretchen grabbed the pistol before I could.

"Give it here, Sis," Robert pleaded while holding his injured arm close to his body.

Gretchen didn't budge. She kept her eyes on the weapon as if unsure what to do next. Would she finish the job for the brother she practically raised and loved like a son? I held my breath and watched her lift the gun, and then after a moment, she lowered it, keeping the weapon close to her side. I rose to my feet and looked around, debating if I should make a run for it. Robert cursed and then grabbed me by the neck with his left hand. "I don't need a weapon to kill her."

"Let go of her, Robert!" Gretchen pleaded. "Or I'll shoot you."

Not willing to put my life in the hands of a tormented woman struggling between friendship or family, I kicked Robert in the shins over and over. He had his arm around my neck, and I raised my hand to scratch him in the eyes as Jack had taught us in a self-defense class, but Robert kept turning his face away. We continued to struggle until suddenly the blast of gunfire filled the air.

CHAPTER EIGHTEEN
"A friend in need is a friend indeed."

———

"I told you to let her go, Robert!" Gretchen's voice shook when she said her brother's name. She had fired into the air, and tears streamed down her face as she lowered the gun in his direction. "I mean it. Don't make me shoot you."

My heart raced, and I felt Robert's arm tense as his hold on my neck tightened. A white cloud filled my peripheral vision, and my legs wobbled.

"You're not going to shoot me," Robert said with a hint of concern in his voice. "Gretchen, you've always had my back. Everything I've done was to keep you happy."

"Killing my friend is not going to make me happy." She kept her voice firm and steady despite her hand trembling.

We'd never spoken of guns before, so as far as I knew, how well she handled a gun was anyone's guess.

"I get it now." He eased his hold on me and let out a sharp laugh. "You don't have to watch. Don't worry, go on back to the car and wait for me there."

"No, Robert," she shouted this time. "I won't let you do this."

However, I never got to find out if Gretchen would have really shot her brother to save me or not because at that moment Jack and Cody came thrashing through the trees with their guns drawn.

"Let her go," Jack ordered in a voice that demanded to be obeyed, "and then put your hands in the air."

Robert cursed and then released me, stepped away, and put his arms in the air. Cody went to Gretchen and gently removed the gun still clasped in her fists.

"Are you all right, Lily?" Jack asked as he holstered his gun, pulled out a pair of handcuffs, and slapped them on Robert's wrists.

"Yes." I didn't mention my throat hurt from the tight hold Robert had had on my neck. The last thing I wanted was a trip to the hospital, which is exactly what my brother-in-law would insist on happening if I were to complain about any ache or pain.

"What's going on here?" Jack's gaze seemed to take in all three of us at once—Robert's glare, Gretchen's tears, and my adrenaline-induced heavy breathing. My heart and lungs felt like I'd just finished running a marathon.

"He killed the accountant," I blurted out between huffs.

And he was going to kill me. I went weak in the knees and felt myself start to wobble. It seemed as if the air had been sucked out of my lungs. The sound of Jack's deep voice reading Robert his rights registered in my brain, but the words sounded far away and muffled.

"Hang on." Cody slipped his strong arm around my waist and held me close. "I've got you. You're okay."

"I'm fine," I managed to mimic, too weak to pull away even if I had wanted to. The warmth from Cody's body calmed my nerves, and I turned my face upward to give him a smile. Warmth radiated from his eyes, and my focus was drawn to the slight grin on his lips as he leaned closer. My heart did a flip-flop, and I felt myself swoon.

Jack cleared his throat. "Why don't we all take a trip to the station where we can figure this out?"

The hike out of the woods didn't take as long as the previous trek meant to silence me. Cody stayed close by my side while Gretchen walked in front of us, following Jack who had her brother in custody. No one said a word as if afraid or unable to break the tension hanging over the group. Unlike before, I noticed birds dipping and diving from branches in the trees, fortifying their nests with new straw-like materials. Squirrels scurried with last minute scavenging to fill their homes with an ample supply of nuts and acorns for the winter. The forest was alive, just like me. Thank God.

When we finally exited the canopy of timbers, the sight of Jack's Crown Vic parked next to my Jeep brought tears to my eyes. The familiar sight was exactly what I needed after my emotional ordeal.

"Gretchen, you can ride in the squad car with your brother and me. Cody, why don't you drive Lily in her Jeep, and we'll have a tow truck pick up the other vehicle."

In full chief of police mode, my brother-in-law took control of the situation.

"You can ride in the back with your brother," Jack said to Gretchen after he helped the prisoner into the vehicle. "Lily, let Cody do the driving."

"What about my car?" Gretchen asked.

"It'll be towed and searched," he said in a gruff voice. I realized until Jack heard the facts, Gretchen was under suspicion, but since he hadn't read her her rights, she wasn't under arrest.

"How did you know where to find me?" I asked Cody once we were alone in the Jeep. "Or that I even needed finding?"

He took his eyes off the road long enough to give me a smile and said, "We were on our way to take a report at the trailer park on Old Quarry Road, but we decided to stop by The Park first and discovered you weren't in the office. No one knew where you were, so we went to the schoolhouse and found Ava."

Ava! My sister must be so worried. I reached for my phone, but it wasn't there. The last time I'd seen my cell phone was when Robert stuck it in his pocket.

"She said you'd both gotten to work early," Cody explained. "Parker was there helping her with the wood stove and informed us he'd seen you leave the parking lot an hour earlier, and you'd turned toward The Grove."

"Thank goodness he saw me leaving." The next time I saw Ava I'd tease her about having her boyfriend hanging out with her during working hours.

"Yes," Cody agreed. "Naturally, we drove out this way to see if you'd broken down or something. We saw your Jeep and Gretchen's car, and when we read the note someone had typed and left in your vehicle, we immediately realized you were in trouble."

Of course, they had to have known the letter was a fake the moment they'd seen it. "I told him no one would believe I wrote that."

Cody reached over and gave my hand a gentle squeeze.

"I really should call Ava," I said. She would worry until she heard from me. "But Robert took my phone."

"Here." Cody took his from his pocket and handed it to me. "You can use mine."

"Where's Lily?" Ava answered before the first ring had time to finish.

"It's me, Ava," I quickly explained. "I'm fine, don't worry."

"Why are you using Cody's phone?" she asked.

"I lost mine." I told a white lie because the truth would only lead to more questions and worry. "I'm going to the station with Jack and Cody."

She let out a gasp. "Either you're being arrested, or you solved the murder mystery."

"Yes," I said, without giving her any details.

"So, who did it?" she demanded.

"I can't talk about it right now," I said. She let out a sharp huff, so I added, "As soon as I get back, I'll tell you everything."

After assuring her I was fine, I hung up and leaned back against the headrest with my eyes closed. It felt good to be alive. Poor Gretchen, she had looked so lost and devastated when Jack helped her into the back of his cruiser.

"Did you find out why Robert killed Mr. Rinehart and how?" Cody asked.

"Yes. Ava and I never suspected Robert." I straightened and cringed at the raspy sound in my throat.

"Why did he do it?" Of course, Cody would need to know all the details.

"When Gretchen's brother asked her to lend him money to pay off a gambling debt, she told him she didn't have the money, but he knew she'd skimmed funds from the petty cash account before."

"And?" The tone in his voice made it clear he wanted me to keep talking.

"She refused to help him," I explained, "and she told him it was impossible to take that much out without being flagged by the auditing system."

"So how did he get the money?" Cody looked adorable when he was confused. His brows stretched out, and his lips thinned.

"That's the puzzling part." I shook my head, taking a moment to try and piece it together enough to make sense. "In September, on the first morning of Gretchen's vacation with her brother, they stopped by the office because she wanted him to meet me before they left town for a retreat they were taking. I wasn't there because I had several tours scheduled and therefore didn't get to meet Robert."

"So, she was supposed to be on vacation when this theft transpired," Cody said. I nodded before he continued, "Was anyone else in the office?"

"Joyce was holding down the fort for us that week," I answered. "She took a quick break since Gretchen could cover her for a little while."

Cody looked thoughtful. "So, Gretchen and her brother hung around the office for a while."

"Yes, they were going to the mountains for a family retreat," I said. "While she was in the restroom, he got into the safe we kept under her desk and took out the cash. Nice of him to only take what he needed, which was one thousand dollars. He said he'd watched her use the money in the safe before to pay people and knew exactly where she hid the key."

Cody pulled up to the tracks and put the Jeep in park while we waited for a train to pass. "Why didn't anyone notice the money was missing sooner?"

"This all took place back in September when we'd had a community fundraiser to purchase a new highway sign," I explained. We had really needed a newer sign. Paint was peeling from the old one, and some of the boards looked rotted. "Donations were coming in left and right, and we'd put them in petty cash for the time being."

"Wow, everything just fell into place for him." Looking doubtful, Cody emphasized the word *him*, but I still believed Gretchen was innocent. "Why didn't Gretchen say something sooner?"

"He didn't tell her about it until the auditor was called in to investigate. When he told her he'd been the one to take the money, Gretchen was furious," I explained in her defense. "She used to date Melvin Rinehart and knew he was the bank's internal auditor. She believed he would connect her excessive shopping habits with the missing money, especially when he saw the money being moved in and out of the petty cash account."

"So, to keep his sister from getting into trouble," Cody said, "he killed the accountant."

"Yes." I rubbed a spot on my forehead that was beginning to throb. The whole thing was a nightmare. I shuddered to think of the times I'd seen Robert when he came to pick up Gretchen for lunch, never realizing he was the killer. "She says she had nothing to do with the murder and didn't know about it until he confessed to her one day while they were at lunch."

"Do you believe her story?" Cody asked just as the last train car passed. He turned on the engine and put the Jeep into drive.

"Yes, I do," I insisted with the same passion in my voice Ava had used to defend her friend, Chloe. How could I have ever thought the sweet, yet spunky hairdresser capable of murder?

Cody stayed silent, so I added, "And not just because she saved my life."

"What I don't understand is why he attacked you today." Cody turned left onto Main Street. We were almost to the station. "He'd already done a fine job of framing you."

"When he went to Melvin's office building, no one was around, and the only person upstairs was the accountant," I explained. "He thought it would be easy to get in and out without any witnesses, but in his rush to leave he'd lost his cufflink."

"Cufflink?" The look of confusion on Cody's face reminded me of the expression Pat gave Ava when she'd mess up a saying.

"Yes," I explained sheepishly. "I found something on the ground on my way to the accountant's office. I thought the thing I picked up was a penny and put it in my purse for Ava to add to her collection."

Cody pulled into the station and drove the car to the back entrance. "How did he find out you had it?"

"One day when he came by the office to pick Gretchen up for lunch, I was showing the cufflink to her to see if she recognized the logo or knew where it came from."

"So." Cody cut off the engine and handed me the keys. "That means he must have been the one inside the basement the night you got hit on the head."

"Yes," I said. "He was looking for the cufflink since it tied him to the scene of the crime."

The hairs on the nape of my neck rose at the memory of Robert showing off my dad's watch. The family heirloom wasn't expensive but held fond memories. We hadn't noticed it missing after the break-in, but I was positive the watch Robert wore belonged to my sisters and me. "He's wearing my father's wristwatch. He must have taken it when he was in the house."

CHAPTER NINETEEN
"Laughter is the best medicine."

———

Less than a month later, Pat and I sat in the den, looking through some furniture magazines while we waited for Ava to finish a class in the basement. When I had quietly suggested we consider redecorating the house, the idea seemed to excite my older sister. I had yet to bring up the subject with Ava. As the youngest and most invested in the house, she would be the hardest to convince. Other than college and the two years she'd lived with her husband before he died, she'd spent all her life in this house. If she had a problem with making changes, we would drop the subject. Her happiness was more important to both Pat and me than a new kitchen set or couch. But just in case, we were looking for ideas.

"All right." Ava came up from the basement and startled us. "We finished early, so I'm ready to help with the planning."

Just over a week away, we'd set up this meeting with Pat to discuss Thanksgiving dinner. With a soda in her hand, Ava took her seat next to mine. "What do you two have so far?"

"We've just been chatting," Pat said as she stuffed the magazine under the folder she had on her lap. "You didn't expect us to start without you, did you?"

"Since when has that ever stopped you before?" Ava looked suspicious and with good reason. Pat never would have made it as an actress.

"We've been looking at furniture." I threw it out there to see her reaction. "Some things around here are getting worn out."

The smile on her face surprised me. "That's a great idea," she said. "I wondered if you two would ever get around to fixing the place up."

"Us?" Pat asked with a huff. "It's as much your place as ours, even more so really."

Happy to have Ava with us, I took on my usual role as peacemaker. "We can talk about what to do later. Right now, we need to figure out Thanksgiving."

"I have to know how many to expect before I can plan how much food we'll need." Pat got out her pen and planning calendar. "Jack, the kids, and I make four, plus the two of you are six. Ava, are you planning to ask anyone to join us this year?"

Holidays had always been a big deal at our house, and our parents had taught us to share the joy. Mom and Dad often had invited friends over who would have otherwise been alone at dinner time.

Ava glanced at me and then Pat. "Lily and I had talked about having Sam Smith over for dinner sometime."

"Thanksgiving would be the perfect time to invite him," I said since he seemed to enjoy kids, and the twins loved attention. Besides, I owed it to him for having my back when he warned me to back off the case. His only concern had been my safety. A lonely old man, he needed friends. "Pat, why don't you see if some of the guys at the precinct will give his shop a try?"

"That's a good idea." She seemed pleased by my suggestion.

Business should pick up for his shop if Pat put in a good word at the station. Her husband may be the chief, but she had a great deal of pull with the officers. Every year, every holiday, Pat had been there with treats and surprises to lift their morale.

"You should take Jack Jr. down there to get his hair cut." Ava smiled, but her words were bittersweet. "He'd love hearing stories about the grandfather he never met."

"I will." Pat sniffed a bit and then held her pen in the air, ready for action. "Anyone else?"

Score one for Ava! To show my gratitude, I'd be sure to fold all the clothes for an entire week.

"What about Chloe?" I looked over at Ava, who was misty-eyed as well. "Does she have plans?"

"She goes to her sister's for the holiday," Ava reminded me. "Also, she's been crazy busy getting ready to move into the larger upstairs office for her salon after the holidays."

"Perfect." Pat smiled and leaned forward to look at me, but Ava cleared her throat and a bit of a blush spread across her cheeks. "I invited Parker, and he's looking forward to joining us."

Pat jotted down his name and looked at Ava as if waiting for more names. After a moment of apparently daydreaming, our younger sister seemed to realize she was in the spotlight and stuttered, "That's all, just those two—Sam and Parker."

"Okay." Pat looked a bit relieved, and I held back a laugh. She loved to cook for people, but too big a crowd might stress her out. "Lily, how about you?"

"I thought about inviting Brynn, but when I called her this morning, I found out she has plans."

"With Ethan?" The way Ava wrinkled her nose, you'd have thought a skunk got loose in the house.

"Haven't you heard?" Actually, I knew she hadn't since I'd just found out myself when I asked Brynn about her plans. "Ethan got his bike fixed and blew town when Brynn discovered the cost of updating the freezer in his ice cream parlor was too expensive. She is doing what her uncle wanted all along and is putting the building up for sale."

"So, what is Brynn doing for dinner?" Pat asked.

"Helping serve food at the mission." I'd come to realize the young woman couldn't sit or stand still for long. Always on the run, it was a good thing she was dedicated to helping others.

"What about Cody?" Pat gave me one of her cheeriest grins, proud matchmaker that she was. "Is he eating with his boys again this year?"

"Christopher and his wife are spending the weekend with her family in Sacramento, and Drake can't get away from college and his work scholarship job," I said, struggling to keep a straight face as I continued. "I guess that means Cody's all on his own this year. Do you think I should ask him to eat with us?"

Pat gave me that wrinkled brow look of hers that she reserved for when one of her kids were trying to get away with something. "You better have already invited him."

"Yes," I said with a grin, "he'll be here."

The sound of bus brakes grinding sounded out front. Pat glanced at the clock on the wall and stood.

"Don't worry." Ava stood too and said, "The front door isn't locked."

Before we could reach the living room, the door flew open, with Jack Jr. and Jill bursting into the house. Pat had instructed the bus driver to bring them to the farm when she put them on the bus this morning.

"Are we ready to go?" Jill hopped up and down with excitement.

Her brother, Jack, who was calmer, looked just as thrilled. "We better hurry before it gets too dark."

Tomorrow was the grand opening of The Park's first zip line ride, but we needed to have a few test runs first. Actually, the ride had been tested and passed inspection. What could I say? Sometimes having your aunt manage a theme park came with perks.

Enjoying my day off, I went to The Park wearing jeans and a sweater. It felt surreal. While Ava and Pat took the kids to the top of the hill, I couldn't help stopping in the office. For an excuse, I said I wanted to lock my purse in my locker rather than chance losing it on the ride. Gretchen sat at the receptionist's desk, filling out worksheets for next week's work roster. She wore a blue sweater over her white blouse and tan slacks. Nothing outlandish, but nice for the office. Apparently the counseling for her addiction was helping. She no longer handled petty cash, and Steve promised to hire a payroll clerk to handle paychecks.

"How's it going?" I asked on my way back from dropping my purse off in my office.

"Fine." Her bright smile had waned since the ordeal with her brother, but she still had a cheerful demeanor. "Are the kids here to try out the ride?"

"Yes, and they are very excited," I said. "I just thought I'd stop in to see if anything needed my attention."

"Nope, everything's fine. You need to go and enjoy your day off, boss." She finished with a wink and a smile.

I rode the tram up to the top of the hill and arrived right before the rest of the crew.

"Are you ready?" I asked the kids.

"You're sure this is safe?" Pat had to raise her voice to be heard over their cheers.

"Don't worry." I tried to calm her motherly concerns. "They're in good hands."

I sat next to Jack Jr., and Ava rode next to Jill. Pat rode the tram to the bottom where we'd meet her.

"Ready or not, here we go," I yelled as the wire gate beneath our feet fell away, and we were airborne. The crisp autumn air brushed against my face, tugging on my hair. Like the experienced zip-liner I was, I'd pulled my curly locks back in a bow.

Spread out below our feet lay the Calico Rock Mine and Ghost Town. From this height, I could see the steeple on top of the church next to the schoolhouse near the cemetery. Down the hill from those two structures, false front buildings lined either side of Main Street. On the end closest to the mine entrance sat the sheriff's office across from the saloon, mercantile, and bank where our weekly stunt shows took place.

"Look at the train." Jack pointed it out to me.

The Park's miniature train filled with riders was halfway up the incline that would give them a view of the river below. Ava, the kids, and I had a blast. When we reached the bottom, Pat was waiting for us.

"Jack and Jill want to go up the hill again." Ava could hardly get the phrase out without giggling.

I couldn't help laughing but told them this was a special trip, and we'd have to wait until we officially opened it to ride again.

We had to stop by the office so I could pick up my things. I left my sister and the kids in the lobby chatting with Gretchen while I got my purse. When I left the office, I locked the door behind me, which was a part of the new protocol. Not that the committee thought anyone would try to steal petty cash from the safe. This way there was no doubt, since the only way anyone other than me could touch it was to break in.

"See you in the morning." I waved to Gretchen and joined my family in the lobby.

"Sometimes I can't help but feel Steve is partial to her," Pat whispered as soon as we left the building. "I understand she's very likable, flaws and all, but still."

"It's because she is a spaz," Ava said.

Pat and I look at each other. I shrugged first.

"What are you talking about?" Pat asked in her most straightforward voice, as if our little sister had lost her mind.

Ava looked frustrated as she repeated herself. "You know, spaz."

"If you mean she has pizzazz," I said, coming to her rescue, "I totally agree with you."

Gretchen had a certain flair about her, and not many people could pull off coming back to work after what she'd been through. Her brother's trial would be coming up next month. Thank goodness we had solved the mystery and could go on with our lives without any more drama and danger in the air.

"Until next time." Jill's words pulled me from my musings. It was as if she'd read my mind.

"What did you say?" I asked, a little startled.

My niece raised her eyes to meet mine and smiled. "I loved the zipline and can't wait until next time."

Relieved that I'd misunderstood her, I took my niece's hand in mine as we walked with the family. "Yes, there will soon be a next time."

ABOUT THE AUTHOR

Jamie L. Adams fell in love with books at an early age. *Little Women* by Louisa May Alcott opened her imagination and sparked a dream to be a writer. She wrote her first book as a school project in 6th grade. Living in the Ozarks with her husband, twin daughters, and a herd of cats, she spends most of her free writing, reading, or learning more about the craft near to her heart.

To learn more about Jamie, visit her online at:
www.jamieladams.com

Made in the USA
Las Vegas, NV
31 March 2024